PAWN

The Pawn Duet, Book Two

TM FRAZIER

Pawn, The Pawn Duet, Book Two

By T.M. Frazier

Copyright @ 2020 by T.M. Frazier

Edited by: Karla Nellenbach, Last Word Editing

Ellie, My Brothers Editor

Cover design & formatting: T.M. Frazier

For my readers

*"The belief that there is only one truth,
and that oneself is in possession of it,
is the root of all evil in the world."*

— MAX BORN

1

MICKEY

TIME TRAVEL IS POSSIBLE.

Not the *Back to the Future*, flux-capacitor, kind of time travel. And not the *Outlander* through-the-stones kind either. Although even in my scientifically fact- oriented mind, I'm still holding out hope for that last one.

But yet, it exists, not out there in the world, but within ourselves.

Time is an intangible unit of measurement that knits together the fabric of the past into a proverbial quilt of memories that make up the timeline of our lives.

Though time itself is a constant, during certain moments it can slow to a crawl or it can blur by like a speeding train.

Emotional reactions can often trigger memories that will transport us in time, to a specific moment on the quilt.

One that is either defined or destroyed.

The research has already been written, but no publication on the subject could've ever prepared me for my own experience with time travel.

Because in one moment, I'm in the warehouse of The

Fourth Reich, unable to believe what I'm seeing before my eyes, and the next, I'm back in the van with my family, careening through the barricade into the cold dark water. Only, there's no splash, and the cold I feel is not coming from around me, but within me, expanding through my body, chilling me to my very core.

Suddenly, I'm jolted from the van, and I'm back in Pike's bed. My body warms as he wraps his heat around me, pulling me close to his chest. I want to stay here, in this place and in this moment. The stubble on his jaw lightly scrapes against my cheek and I'm filled with regret for ever having left him.

Pike's arms leave me all too soon, and I'm tossed back into the cold, but this time, it's courtesy of the water that was just poured over my head from behind. I watch as my three younger sisters take off down the beach, carrying with them a now empty bucket, and the sweet sounds of their childish laughter. Even under the warm sun, the breeze chills the water on my skin.

I shiver.

I continue to bounce around to different junctures of my own timeline. Some sweet and warm. Others heartbreaking and chilling.

Several times, I find myself in moments with Pike. Moments that took place over the last few weeks. It seems like such a small period of time, but three weeks is all it took for me to fall in love with Pike. Three weeks for my heart to shatter. Three weeks to glimpse the kind of life I'll never have.

Because I did what I thought was right, choosing my plans for revenge and his safety over staying and choosing him.

At least, it had felt like I was choosing him at the time, but now, reliving moments of the recent past, I'm no longer sure that's what I did.

Revenge has been what's propelled me forward going on five years now. Who am I without revenge?

Alone.

That's what I am without it.

But in an instant, a pull of a single thread on my timeline, the plan has changed.

Famous physicist Leonard Susskind once said, "Unforeseen surprises are the rule in science, not the exception. Remember: stuff happens."

I've come to expect surprises in my research, and even in my life, but nothing—and I do mean *nothing*—could have prepared me for this moment. For this surprise.

For my sister to be *alive*.

That thought brings me back into the present, back to the truth that's staring up at me through the rusty bars of a small cage.

A sudden rush of dizziness and confusion, mixed with a feeling of overwhelming euphoria, take hold of me. Closing my eyes tightly, I will the excitement growing in my chest to subside because this can't be real.

She can't be real.

It's just another delusion, Mickey.

I open my eyes and rapidly blink away the blur. She's still here.

My sister is *alive*.

M...Mi...Mickey? Mindy mouths the words, pressing her hand against her throat to indicate that she can't speak. She tries again, but still, sound or not, my name on her lips knocks the wind from my lungs.

Mindy touches her cracked, trembling lips with her fingers. Her arm is caked in dirt and varying colors of bruises, ranging from dark purple to yellow.

Kneeling, I lean in closer. I wrap my hands around the cold bars of the cage. Tears fall from my eyes. If this is just another figment of my imagination, it's both a great and terrible one.

Shaky hands reach out toward me, Mindy brushes a dirty, thin finger across my knuckle, sucking in a breath at the contact. The feeling of her touch lights up my senses and makes me temporarily dizzy. She quickly withdraws her touch as if pulling her hand from a flame.

"It really is you," I whisper, looking over this new older, yet broken version of my sister. I try and pull the door open, but it's locked. I look around for a key or something to pry it open, but I don't see anything in my immediate view. "We've got to get you out of here," I tell her.

She shakes her head and cowers back to the other side of the cage as if she expected me to be as imaginary as she's been in my life for years. But the reason I know she's real isn't just because of her touch but because all of the millions of times I've imagined my family, conjured them like imaginary spirits to stand before me and keep me company in the lonely world I've created for myself, they've always appeared to me the same. Healthy. Whole.

Nothing at all like the shattered human being caged before me.

My throat feels thick and dry with unshed sobs. I'm balancing the weight of the world on my chest, and I feel it pushing against my rib cage and threatening to crush my already fragile heart. If this is some sort of game—some sort of new mental breakdown I've not experienced before— don't know how I can get over it.

"What happened to you?" I ask, trying to steady my voice

the same way one would when coaxing a frightened animal from hiding. "How is it possible that you're here?"

Tears well up in her red-rimmed eyes. She pushes a stiff strand of hair from her face that falls right back into place. She crawls forward slowly until we're eye to eye. She smells like feces and something putrid, but I don't care because she's real and she's here. She tentatively wraps her hands around mine, which are white-knuckling the bars. We both take in deep, shaky breaths. She's silent for a moment, but after she looks me over again, her eyes meet mine.

She opens her mouth to speak.

The words don't get a chance to leave her mouth because the loud crash of the door opening startles us both. She leaps back into the corner of her cage as several heavy footsteps cross over the concrete. She's shaking violently. I place my finger to my lips, and she nods. I crawl slowly and quietly behind the cage, fitting myself behind a pair of empty beer kegs.

A crack of separation between the barrels gives me a small view of Percy and Darius as they approach. "What the fuck is this, old man?" Percy asks, waving his hand at the cage where my sister is pretending to be asleep.

"This is a gift. For your wife," Darius announces proudly. "From you."

Percy scratches his bald head. "Okay, but why?" He lights a cigarette.

Darius wags his finger at Percy, then crouches down to admire his captive. "Because she will love it. Because it will make you a hero to her to give her the gift of a life. You know how she's always rescuing things. Injured birds, stray fucking cats. Now, she's not the only one. You're now a rescuer and, therefore, more relatable. Loveable, even. A perfect gift."

"And why is that?" Percy asks, crossing his arms over his chest.

Darius places his hand on Percy's shoulders. "You are going to be a married man, and more importantly, the future leader of The Reich. You need to exercise control in every situation. You and Michaela have known one another since you were children in The Reich, but you don't know each other as man and wife. Not yet. I see how you two interact with one another. You act like complete strangers."

Percy scoffs. "Yeah, but you ever think that's because we haven't seen each other since I got locked up? She was just a kid then. I was just a fucking teenager. We don't know each other as adults. And I don't know, but maybe, because having an arranged marriage doesn't exactly make shit any less awkward?"

"Exactly, this is a fresh start between you. If not a fresh start, then consider this a lesson in control. Use this gift to influence your new wife. Threaten her with it when you have to. Kill it in front of Mickey if and when the time calls for it."

Referring to my sister as *it* has me balling my fists and clenching my jaw with rage. How can they speak so casually about the life of my sister as if she was nothing more than a rodent?

Percy widens his stance and takes a deep drag of his cigarette, flicking the ashes too close to the cage. "I've been locked up for a while, so forgive me 'cause I'm not really seeing the value in this."

Darius pats his shoulders, then removes his hands, taking a step back. "You can thank me later when you understand. Trust me, there will come a time when you'll need to utilize her. There always is."

Percy looks down at the cage, then back up to Darius.

"So, you want me to keep her in a cage until such a time arises?" He sniffs the air. "The smell of piss and shit is burning my fucking eyes."

Darius slaps him on the back of the head. "No, moron. I would assume that your wife would not want to keep her in the fucking cage. Clean her up before you give her to Mickey. I don't think she'd be too happy to see her in this pathetic state."

"What if she's not healthy? Mickey's not gonna be happy if she dies seconds after I let her out of the cage," Percy muses. "And she ain't looking so good."

"Do I have to do all of your thinking for you, too?" Darius sighs. "Have her looked at. If she's not up to making your wife happy, take her to an open field and put a bullet in her fucking head. Mickey will never know you even had her to begin with." His heavy footsteps echo as does the slam of the door to the warehouse as it closes behind him.

"Thanks for fucking nothing, Pops," Percy mutters, leaning on the cage and peering inside. My sister's leg twitches against the bars.

Percy jumps back and wipes his palms together. He inspects her again and finds that she's sleeping. He sighs and takes another drag off his cigarette.

He removes his phone from his pocket and presses a few buttons, walking to the far corner of the warehouse where I can't make out who he's talking to, nevermind what he's saying.

It doesn't matter. There's no time to decipher his call. What I need right now is a weapon.

Cold concrete chills my skin as I crawl to the other side of the warehouse. Mindy opens her eyes as I pass the cage. I press my finger over my lips. I know she understands what

I'm telling her because she closes her eyes again, continuing to fake sleep. Above me is a tower of shelving reaching all the way to the ceiling. Without standing up and drawing attention to myself, I carefully feel around the first dusty shelf until I finally wrap my hand around something I know I can use.

Gingerly, I lift the crowbar from the shelf and tuck it against my chest, crawling back across the warehouse as fast as I can, but it's hard without using the hand clutching my newfound weapon. My thigh pulses and stings as my self-inflicted bullet wound tears open. I grit my teeth against the pain. Warm, fresh blood drenches the bandage wrapped around my leg.

I manage to tuck myself back behind the kegs just as Percy reappears, shoving his phone into his back pocket.

My breathing is shallow and quiet as I wait for the perfect moment. He squats down to again peer at my sister.

It's now or never.

Rising to my feet, I lift the crowbar in the air just as the door flies open and I'm forced to drop back down.

"What the fuck you need, P?" asks a masculine voice I recognize as Hoppy, Percy's friend and one of the higher-ranking members of the Reich.

"You know anything about this?" Percy asks, waving his hand to the cage.

Hoppy smiles. "Sure did," he answers proudly. "What do you want me to do with her?"

"Well, since she's a gift, I guess I gotta fix the fucking packaging," Percy replies. "Move her out of this hot-ass ware-house and call Knox. Tell him to bring his medical kit and ask him to look her over and see what needs fixin'. I'll have Mary bring her some food and water."

Hoppy eyes him suspiciously. "P?" he asks, as if he

somehow misunderstood his orders. I can't pretend that I'm not disappointed by not getting to kill Percy today, but I also can't deny the relief I feel that Mindy will be treated properly, at least until I can get her the fuck out of here. Besides, it will be easier to break her out of a locked room than a locked cage.

Percy raises his voice, clearly irritated. "I can't give my wife damaged goods, can I?" he asks. "Tell me, Hop, would you give your old lady a dress with a fucking hole in it or a ring missing a stone?"

Hoppy shakes his head. "Nah, man. I'd get the couch for sure. That is, if I had an old lady."

Percy crosses his arms over his bare, tattooed chest. "Well then, tell me if you think it's a good idea to give Mickey a gift that's all banged up and half-starved to death?" He looks at my sister. "In a fucking cage?"

"Yeah, that won't be no good." Hoppy shakes his head and rubs his protruding belly, satisfied with Percy's explanation. "No good at all. Good call, man. See, this is why you're the smart one. You'll make a good leader, P."

"Just tell me what Knox says," Percy orders.

Hoppy wheels over a large cart. Locking the brakes, he parks it next to the cage. He lifts it without much effort and sets it on the cart.

"Nobody is to know about this. Not even members. Are we clear?" Percy points his finger sternly at Hoppy.

"Clear as...well...some shit that's clear." Hoppy shakes off his hands and follows Percy out of the room with my sister in tow. "What then? What are you gonna do if Knox doesn't give her all the all-clear? She don't look too fucking good."

Percy opens the door, allowing Hoppy to wheel through.

"Then, I'll load my fucking shotgun."

The door slams shut, and I'm left alone in the dark.

My entire body is shaking.

The plan has changed. Revenge be damned. There is only one plan now.

I have to get to my sister.

Before *they* do.

2

PIKE

OVER THE PAST TWENTY-FOUR HOURS, I've switched back and forth between the need to drive to the compound and put a bullet in the head of everything and everyone with a heartbeat and a deep burning desire to just forget everything that's happened over the past few weeks. I could sell my fucking pawn shop, and drive to the furthest corner of the country, leaving it all in the fucking rearview mirror of my truck.

The problem with that plan is that Mickey's memory can't be left behind with everything else. Because I know that no matter how hard I try, I'll never get her off my brain. My chest tightens. Or off my fucking chest. The weight of Mickey leaving without so much as a, *See you the fuck later, Pike. It's been real but I'm going back to the fucking racists*, crushes me over and over again like a car falling off its jack, trapping me underneath.

A soft meowing penetrates my thoughts. The longer I ignore the sound, the louder it gets, but ignoring the creature is what I want to do because it only reminds me of Mickey, down on the ground in the alley tending to the strays like they were well-respected members of her family.

Family she doesn't have because they're all fucking dead.

Hence her need for revenge on the Fourth Reich and the very reason why she left. Why, in a way, she chose them over me.

If that's even the truth.

Trust is something I've never been fucking good at, but what fucking sets fire in my fucking veins is that I wanted to trust Mickey. I still want to. But the growing doubt grows with each passing hour, twisting into a spark of rage.

Besides, I'd be stupid if I didn't think there was a small possibility that Mickey played me, and her entire charade, including the show she put on in my bed, was all for the benefit of an easier escape back to her people.

No, that part wasn't a show. You can't fake what we had in my bed. Her response to my touch.

I shake my head. Just because she liked it when I made her come doesn't mean she didn't lie about the rest. It means she's human.

She could still be one of them.

"Fuck!" I yell into my empty apartment, emptier now that Mickey isn't here filling it with her constant need to try and figure me out. I chuckle, remembering when she made the observation about my learning disorder. I looked up her diagnosis, and she was right. About all of it. About me.

Too bad I may not have been right about her.

The meowing continues, at a faster and louder pace. The feline equivalent of, *you can't ignore me forever!*

"Fuck, alright, hang the fuck on!" I yell. Leaving my bottle of whiskey, I pad over to the door, cracking it open. I head back to the couch, plopping down onto the well-worn leather. Plucking the whiskey bottle from the table, I tip it back and take a long—much needed—pull.

The source of the meowing jumps up onto my lap and positions itself so that its little grey and white striped paws are on my chest, its apple-shaped head resting below my chin. It weighs no more than a couple of pounds and is no bigger than my Glock 43. The tiny creature looks up at me with a runny nose and even runnier eyes. It meows again, the sound vibrating against my chest.

I sigh. "I know. She's gone. I don't know what the fuck to do about it either," I say, scratching it behind the ears.

My explanation apparently isn't good enough for the scrawny little thing because suddenly its claws dig into skin through my shirt. I leap to my feet with the whiskey bottle still in my hand, but the thing doesn't let go, it only sinks its little talons deeper, hanging off my shirt and essentially from my skin like a little fuzzy parasite. Shaking it off doesn't work either and only earns me a hiss.

"Are we interrupting an interpretive dance recital?" Nine asks from the open doorway. "Because I don't remember you telling me you were taking dance lessons."

"Interpretive dance is overrated," Preppy chimes in, pushing past his younger brother into the room. "It's all about theatrical dance now."

"And how would you know that?" Nine asks, stepping into the kitchen as Preppy takes a seat on the couch, draping a leg over the armrest.

Preppy scoffs. "How does one not fucking know that?"

I grab hold of the back of the kitten's neck and yank, successfully managing to detach it from both my skin and my shirt. It hisses again, and I hiss back. "Fucking prick," I swear.

That earns me another hiss.

"What's with the cat?" Nine asks, opening the fridge and pulling out a beer. He uses the edge of the counter to pop the top off with his fist. "New friend?"

I cross the room and set the thing back out in the hallway. I kick the door shut behind me. I'll take the fucking relentless meowing over being shanked with twenty tiny shives.

Nine raises his eyebrows and points to my shirt. I look down to find it's pebbled with droplets of blood. "Little fucker," I mutter, pulling off my shirt and throwing it on the counter. I take another swig from the bottle, and then another, and another, until I've swallowed several mouthfuls. I wipe my mouth with the back of my hand as my throat burns and blood drips down my chest.

"You need an AA meeting or something?" Preppy asks, eyeing the now half-empty bottle.

"You, of all people, need to be asking that question?" I spit back. I take a seat on the recliner and rest the bottle on my knee.

"Touchy, are we? Besides, I can ask you that because I'm not an addict. I'm a party opportunist. There's a difference." Preppy pulls out a large bag of blow from his pocket and dips a key from his keychain inside. He closes one nostril and snorts it. He, then, holds out the key to me. "Bump?"

"I'll pass. I'm not really in the mood to feel alert."

Nine chuckles. "Party opportunist? This ain't exactly a party, Prep."

Preppy sniffs, shoving the bag back into his shirt pocket. He holds his nostrils shut and then sniffles again, shaking his head rapidly from one side to the other. "Yes, party opportunist." He points to himself, Nine, and then me. "We have three people, booze, and blow. I see the opportunity for a party, and I take it."

Nine rolls his eyes. "So, can we get back to the cat? What the fuck was up with that?"

I scratch my chin. "It's nothing. Just a fucking cat."

"Liar," Nine says, snatching the bottle from my hand. He pours a large amount into a glass and hands it to me as if it will somehow slow me down. He sets the bottle back on the counter. "I know Mickey loved those fucking alley cats. Is that why you got one of them up here?"

"It was supposed to be a gift," I reluctantly admit. "For Mickey. That one was always on her lap. She hated to leave it out there, and the little thing would always wait for her at... I shake off the memories. "It was a dumb fucking idea. Doesn't matter now."

"Yeah, it was a dumb idea. Bitches don't want cats," Preppy chuckles. "Cats are too much of an obvious choice when considering domestic pet options."

Nine points his beer at Preppy, "Says the man with a pet pig."

Preppy points an accusing, tattooed finger at Nine. "You leave the sacred name of my Oscar out of this. He's better company than either of you sniveling little shits. And Bear has a fucking coyote. So, there's that." He sits up. "Okay, let's talk about the real reason why we are here. Like the fact that it's been twenty-four hours since you called off plans for us to storm The Fourth Reich compound, and we have no immediate plans on the calendar to kill them at all, and why you're wallowing up here like an old, fucking cat lady."

I raise an eyebrow at him.

"Trust me, it's true. I know a lot of old cat ladies, and what you're doing up here would be an insult to lovely old cat ladies everywhere."

"I'm not wallowing," I argue, even though I'm not really sure what wallowing means, but I make a note to look it up after these fuckers leave me in peace. "And one cat does not a cat-lady make."

"Seriously, we need to talk," Nine says, looking way too serious and in focus when I was really aiming for more of a drunken blur.

"So, fucking talk," I say, chugging my drink, then setting the empty glass on my knee. "I ain't fucking stopping you." The faster they talk, the faster they leave, and the faster I can get back to my plans of getting shit-faced and wondering when my life had turned to complete and utter shit.

Shit. I think that's what wallowing means.

Preppy takes a deep breath and straightens his bow-tie. He hooks his thumbs under his matching suspenders. "So, I hate to be the one to tell you..."

"What?" I bark, growing irritated. "Spit it the fuck out."

"I hate to be the one to tell you that it's possible that Mickey is a big, fat, lying cunt bucket, and the bitch has to die?" He raises the pitch of his voice and at the end he sounds as if he's been sucking on helium.

"It's not like I haven't thought of the possibility," I grumble. It doesn't make it any easier hearing it cross Preppy's lips or to know that I'm not the only one who has these doubts.

"He's got a point," Nine chimes in. "We know the facts about Mickey's father. About who he was, and about him founding the Reich with Darius. We know they're true because we verified those facts. What we don't know is if the other parts of her story were a lie. The reasons she gave us for her affiliation with The Reich. The revenge. The part about her growing up around them but not believing in their teachings." Nine looks about as reluctant to be having this conversation as I am. "The part where she's with them, but she's not really one of them."

"I have a solution," Preppy announces. He stands and grabs the whiskey bottle from the counter and takes a long drink on his way back to the couch. He plops back down and makes a satisfactory sound. He wipes a piece of lint from his khaki pants. "So, Pike, what you need to do is fuck her, and then, kill her. That way, she's out of your system before you send her out of this world. Problem motherfucking solved." He swipes his palms together, wiping them free of my problems, which he in no way has motherfucking solved.

If only it were that easy, but nothing involving Mickey has been easy or clear. Not even my feelings for her.

After spewing those words, anyone else would be laughing or smiling, because they wouldn't be serious. Not Preppy, but I should know better by now. He's all business, leaning forward on his elbows, his yellow plaid bow-tie as straight as ever, looking more than satisfied with his offered solution.

Nine pushes off the counter and sits next to Preppy on the worn leather couch. He slaps his brother on the back. "Points for creativity, Prep, but I don't think that's exactly the kind of advice that Pike's looking for right now."

He lifts his hands, palms facing up. "What do you mean? What kind of advice doesn't he want? Solid advice? Great advice? Advice from the one and only Samuel Motherfucking Clearwater?" He looks to me. "Is that not what you're looking for?" Preppy's jaw drops, horrified that I would reject his genius.

"Nine's right," I reply, again volleying around feelings of hurt and disappointment and rage at having to discuss the possibility that Mickey betrayed me. That this was all a game to her.

That I was a game.

Preppy sits back and crosses a leg over his knee. His index finger and thumb resting on his chin, his lips twisted in thought. He snaps his fingers, and his eyes light up. "How 'bout this? You kill her first, and *then* fuck her. It's not my bowl of blow, but I'm not going to be all judgey if fucking dead bitches is your thing." He shrugs. "Some people are really into feet."

I close my eyes and hold the cold glass to my temple. "I just need to think about what my next step should be. And no offense, Prep, but necrophilia ain't my thing."

A memory of Mickey warm, naked, and very much alive in my bed floods through my mind. My eyes snap open, not wanting to relive that moment for one second longer.

Now is not the fucking time, I scold myself.

Nine is staring at me with concern written all over his face and it's making me uncomfortable as all hell. He looks down, picking at a loose thread from the seam of the armrest. "We shouldn't have let her go. It's as much my fault as yours. She should have been locked up. I should have told you to keep her locked up until we knew for sure she was telling the truth." The disappointment in his voice is a hard pill to swallow because none of this is his fault. It's mine and *we* didn't let her go. She left. If anyone is to blame, it's me. "What if she had something to do with Gutter getting killed? You took her out there to the swamp right? She met him? What if she told them where he was and how much he meant to you? What if it was her idea…"

His words trail off as the thought sinks in, but I don't have to hear them to know exactly what he's saying and it hadn't occurred to me before that she could have something to do with Gutter's death.

The entire time she was comforting me after he was killed, is it possible that none of that was real? That she planned everything? Knew it was fucking coming?

I look up at Nine whose waiting for my response. "Check my computers downstairs before you leave." I toss him my phone. "This, too. Check deleted search history. See if you can hack the phone records of all calls made out of this building, bar included, to see if you can find any sort of proof that Mickey was communication with The Reich."

"Now, that I can do," Nine says, fingers flying over the keys. He tucks my phone in his pocket. "Hacker to the rescue."

Gutter's face as he told me he loved me right before meeting his end by way of crowbar to the back of his head flashes through my mind. My jaw tightens and so does my grip on the glass. It shatters in my hand.

Nine stands to help me, but I wave him off. "I'm fucking fine." I stand and brush the glass to the floor, scraping and cutting my chest and fingers in the process. It doesn't matter. I can't feel them over the pain inside my chest. The rage. Besides, a few additional cuts can be solved with a Band-Aid. The larger ones can be solved with some Gorilla glue and booze.

The gnawing doubt sawing its way through my fucking heart can't be fixed quite as easy.

If at all.

Glass crunches and slices into my feet as I pad into the kitchen and grab another bottle of whiskey. I return to the couch, rip open the top, and take another healthy pull.

Nine sits back down.

Preppy clears his throat. "Nine's right. You guys shouldn't have let her go. That was never one of the options. Marry or kill. That was it. Did you even read *The Kidnappers Commandments*? I spent a lot of time on that, you know, and not just writing it. I had to break into The Copy Store to print that thing, and that wasn't exactly easy when the Trekkie who runs the printing press holds his Dungeons and Dragons meetings there at night. I was a fucking elf on a quest for six fucking weeks until I was able to sneak away and get it printed." He sighs and looks to the ceiling with regret in his eyes. "I never even got a chance to find the diary of Princess Elfington and release its powers back into the world, restoring the basic rights and magical powers to all of the little elven boys and girls throughout The Kingdom of CopyStoreland."

"I read your shit," I offer. Not only did I read it, but so did Mickey. I catch myself about to smile, remembering the shock on her face when she found Preppy's oddly worded manifesto on the passenger seat of my truck.

Preppy nods. "Okay, then you should know the rules. You didn't marry her, so the bitch has got to go." He takes a joint from the pocket of his button-down and lights it. "And, just to clarify, you know by *go* I mean you gotta kill her."

"Yeah, I think we understood you the first time," Nine says, plucking the joint from Preppy's hand and taking a deep drag.

Preppy snatches it back. "Well, I like to be as clear as possible. The key to good relationships is good communication." He passes me the joint.

I take a deep drag and allow the smoke to burn down my throat into my lungs. Maybe, if I get as high as possible, I'll come up with a solution to all this shit. Worst case scenario, at least, I might be able to fall asleep tonight without dreaming about Mickey.

Nine raises an eyebrow at his brother.

"What?" Preppy gives him a one shoulder shrug. "I'm reading a few relationship books here and there. I want to be able to keep my woman happy both in and out of the sex swing. You should give them a try. Maybe, Poe will like you better."

"She likes me just fine," Nine argues.

"Something wrong with Poe?" I ask. "I thought you said she'd stopped drinking."

"Everything's fine." Nine scratches at the stubble on his jaw. "Preppy just assumes that any girl who is with me doesn't really like me."

"You're just not as sexy as I am. It's okay to live the rest of your life in my shadow. It's a great place to live. Very roomy. High crime rate, but the food and blow are excellent," Preppy ruffles his brother's hair.

Nine responds with an elbow to Preppy's side.

"How...forward thinking of you," Nine says, carefully choosing his words. "To be reading books about how to please your woman."

"I'm nothing if not ever evolving and learning new things." He looks to me and blows out a long stream of smoke into the air. "Now, if I can just get Pikey boy here to understand that he got played, we can get to digging a hole, and my job here will be done."

"We don't know that yet," I argue, turning the bottle around on my knee.

Preppy leans forward, his elbows on his knees. "Hear me out. Mickey's a snitch. She admitted as much to the both of you. She talked to the FEDS about Percy and wore a wire while he was in jail. A snitch who also admits to manipulating the Logan's Beach equivalent of the fucking Klan for her own purposes for years, and if that isn't true, it means you, Pike, are the one she's been manipulating. A snitch, who although is smart, loses her mind on occasion and either thinks her family is still alive, or talks to apparitions she sees before her? How am I doing so far?"

Nine and I exchange looks that say, *Well, he's not wrong.*

Preppy continues. "It's simple. Mickey played you, and she's a snitch, and according to the rhyme, at the very least, she needs to get a beat-down, because you know, snitches get — "

"Stitches," Nine finishes. "We know how it goes."

"It can't be simpler than laid out for you in rhyme format, yet I'm still not sure you two boys are fully comprehending what I'm trying to say here. Shall I put it in a song?" Preppy clears his throat. "Me, me, me, me, motherfuuucking meeeeeeee…."

I raise my hand to stop him before his warm-up leads to a song I won't be able to get him to stop singing or worse, out of my head. Preppy is a crazy fucker who lives by his own set of misguided rules with no reasons behind them that anyone else can figure out, except maybe his wife, but one thing he is, is loyal. Another thing that I can't get past is that everything he said is right. Mickey did snitch on Percy. She even thinks the reason her family was killed could somehow tie back in to her wearing that wire while Percy was in prison. But, why would she admit all of that to us if it wasn't true? And why go back to the Reich if she thinks there is even a possibility that they know about her deception?

The only thing that makes sense is that none of this makes any sense.

Yet, after everything Preppy has just said, I still feel the overwhelming need to defend her. To protect her. "She snitched when she was just a kid, and it was only on Percy. Nine and I both know that fucker had it coming. Kid always had a few screws loose, even way back in juvie."

Preppy cocks his head to the side. "Okay, with that reasoning in mind, let me ask you this: would you or could you snitch on someone when you were fourteen? Ever even consider it?"

When I was fourteen, I was deep into dealing and building my own business on the streets. I'd already made a name for myself, and I knew the rules of the game I was playing. The code of honor amongst thieves. The answer is simple, yet so fucking hard to admit. "No."

Preppy continues, "And, again, with that reasoning still in mind, would you say that you are someone who has on occasion done some questionable and possibly highly illegal things that in the mind of society as a whole would say deserves to be snitched on?"

I sigh because I know what he's getting at. "Yes."

"And she's a genius, right. A professor of psychology, or some shit, right?" Preppy asks, folding his hands together. "A mind master?"

"Doctor," I correct.

"Even better. So she's a *doctor* of psychology. Therefore she knows how the mind works. How it responds. You might even say that she has a degree in manipulation. Sure, she claims to have been using her powers to fuck over the Reich, but what says that she isn't using that shit on you, too? Even if she's not playing on their side, there's nothing to prove that she's playing on yours, besides her word, which I have proven here today to be unreliable bullshit."

"I like you better when you're spewing nonsense," I admit, tired of this line of thought and the fact that I even have to think about them.

Preppy slaps his hands on his thighs, rubbing at his khaki pants. "Well, there you have it, my friend." He counts, ticking off his fingers as he goes. "She snitched." Finger down. "She tried to rob you." Finger down. "She played a part in jacking your shit and attempting to turn King against you." Finger down. "She lives with Neo Nazis, and has their mark burned into her shoulder. She's chanted their chants and walked their walks since childhood." Finger down. "And last, but certainly not least, she left you just when you found out who she really was and that her father was a founding member, which she claims to not have known, but how the fuck wouldn't she know that?" There are no more fingers left on his hand. He opens his fist and wiggles his fingers, pointing to them. "These little piggies don't lie, my friend, and they've decided that she doesn't exactly sound like wifey material. He sits back with his hands resting at the nape of his neck. "The motherfucking prosecution rests." He purses his lips. "Never thought I'd say that one. Heard it a bunch of fucking times from the other side of the courtroom though."

I look to Nine and then at Preppy, feeling both enraged and defeated. "You know, I've been fighting battles and losing at every turn, and I'm so fucking sick of it. It's time to make a few changes."

"That's the spirit!" Preppy cheers, slapping me on the shoulder. "A little homicide will make you feel as right as fucking rain. I'm practically a doctor. I would know."

I laugh at what I was going to tell Mickey before I found my apartment empty and realized she was gone. It seems ridiculous now. "I can't believe I was going to tell her that I'd help her get her revenge and get her out of the Reich." As much as I want to hate Mickey, I can't. It's just not there, and it won't be until I have proof that she's a fucking manipulative liar.

"You should still do it," Nine pipes in. His eyes are wide as he leaps up and paces the room, the glass crunching under his boots. "You should still tell her that you're going to help her."

"What?" Preppy and I ask at the same time.

Nine stands behind the recliner, resting his hands on the high back. "You should still offer to help her get her revenge. Worst case scenario, she'll tell you no, that she doesn't want your help, and then you'll know it's because she's protecting the Reich. You'll know she's been lying this whole time because she's one of them. If she is lying, you'll get your revenge on both the Reich and her."

"A hundred racists with one fucking stone," Preppy chimes in, looking more than a bit baked, his eyes red and veined. "I knew you got some of those smart genes that I got. I was beginning to doubt it for a while there, brother."

Nine rolls his eyes at his brother. Nine is the best hacker around. He speaks computer code better than he does the English language. He ain't exactly dumb.

Nine's idea sinks into my alcohol-riddled brain. I don't hate it. "What's the best case?" I ask, needing to hear it out loud to properly process what I'm getting into here.

"Stitches?" Preppy asks, twisting his lips. "You know, because—"

Nine waves him off. "Yes, we've established that." He rounds the couch and sits at the edge of the cushion. "The best-case scenario is that she agrees to your help, and she's not lying, and we take the fuckers down that killed Gutter. Either way, The Reich falls."

"Don't forget about the drug jacking, the attempt to alienate Pike from King, and the kidnapping of King's daughter by manipulating the biological baby mama during a fucking hurricane," Preppy says, sucking in a large gulp of air when he's done rattling off all the reasons that Percy and Darius are going to die. "'Cause you know King will want in on that, too."

"What he said," Nine agrees.

Nine's right. Before I do anything, I have to find out what side Mickey is on. What her plan is. Her end game.

Preppy snatches the whiskey bottle from my lap. "Either way, it still ends with a little murder-in-the-first and possibly a little necrophilia. Who knows what could happen? It's a crazy world we're living in, but I'd say it sounds like a mother-fucking win for all. Oh, except for the dead guys." He smiles and raises the bottle in the air. "But, they'll be dead, so whatevs."

The lingering fog I've been feeling shifts back into some-thing familiar, something I can work with. Something I can use.

Pure unadulterated rage.

Now I understand why Mickey's quest for revenge is so important to her.

It feels good. To think about it. To imagine it. Shit, tonight I'll probably dream about it.

"So, we all agree then. And after we sort out the Mickey situation, we'll need some intel before we go in there all guns-a-blazing. We'll need a better plan than we had last time. It needs to be cleaner. More precise. We'll need to know how many guards they have. Shift changes and at what time. Weapons stockpiles."

Preppy smiles brightly. "Agreed. Then, we will have

ourselves a big, racist BBQ. I heard hate mongrels taste like chicken."

"If Mickey doesn't want my help, then she isn't going to be our man on the inside. If that's the case, we'll need to send in someone else," I say, suddenly soberer than I've been in the past twenty-four hours.

"Who?" Preppy asks. "Whoever we send, it can't be me. I've got enough issues. Doc will burn my ball hairs off if I tell her I've decided to take up racism as a hobby. She's still mad about all the gear I had custom-made for the Quidditch team I never started taking up all the space in the garage."

I nod. "It has to be someone they won't suspect. Someone they won't know and someone who will fit in."

Nine twists his lips. "It can't be any of us, King, or Bear. Smoke could probably do it, he's great with that kind of shit, but he's out of town with Frankie on a job."

"So, who then?" I ask, wracking my brain of someone we know who is trustworthy enough to penetrate the Reich and ballsy enough to risk their lives and feed us intel.

Preppy pulls out his phone. "Don't worry, boys. I've got this one covered." He steps out into the hall with his phone to his ear. He closes the door, but we can still hear his muffled voice on the other side along with a loud meow.

"Oh, hey kitty-kat. Do you want to join my Quidditch team? Hey, it's Prep," he says to the person on the other line. "Well, hello to you, too, you fucking ray of black sunshine. No, wait! Don't hang up. I need your help. Well, I might need your help. Fuck you, I don't fucking like you either. Was kind of hoping you wouldn't answer on the account of accidentally blowing yourself up or some shit. Regardless of what others might say, I don't find you the least bit attractive. As a matter of fact, I think you're pretty gross. Okay, no wait. I'm sorry. I do think you're mildly pretty, but only when you're not around me. No, fuck, listen! I got a possible job for you, and I promise we can throw knives at each other when it's all done, and everyone is dead. No, you don't get to choose the knives. Okay. Of course, I'll sanitize them beforehand. What kind of fucking monster do you take me for?" His footsteps and voice fade as he makes his way down the stairs.

Nine looks at the door, shaking his head. He frowns. "If Mickey really turns out to be one of them?" He doesn't need to elaborate. He's asking me if I'm willing to carry out the plan and do what needs to be done when the time comes. He's asking me if it comes down to it, will I be able to kill Mickey.

The thought makes me fucking sick, but the reasons why I'd have to kill her make me feel even sicker.

I look my oldest friend in the eye and tell him the painful fucking truth.

"If she's one of them…she will die like one of them."

3

MICKEY

OUR ACTIVITIES in the Fourth Reich weren't real. That's what I grew up believing anyway. Sure, we were there every summer, but our presence and participation were thought to be merely a joke between both scholars and family.

A shared understanding that our membership was for the greater good. For education. To better the world through the information my father was gathering.

To better understand hate.

But what my sisters and I viewed as outsiders trespassing into a dark world for the sake of knowledge, wasn't a lie after all. The only lies were the ones my father told in order to get my family to participate. He was a founder. Nine showed me the picture of him and Darius. Together. Smiling. Proud of what they created together. To my father it was all real. To the members of the Reich—to Darius, Percy and my father—it *is* all real.

I was just too far removed to see it before, but now, glaring at the Fourth Reich brand on my shoulder in the mirror, and thinking about all of the other symbols of hate lining the walls of the compound. Percy's tattoos. The hateful chants. My sister in a cage.

My stomach rolls.

Leaning over the toilet, I pull my hair out of the way just in time. I aggressively purge the contents of my stomach over and over again. If only it was this easy to purge the contents of my soul, sending the dark parts away forever with a simple flush.

Papa was living his truth while the rest of us were caught up in his hateful life of lies. I know why he lied. My mother, who opted to stay at home rather than use her Harvard law degree, would have never participated in this kind of hatred, but she would never back down from an experiment, especially when it could possibly mean a better and less racist world in the end.

The person I looked up to most in the world was a fucking hateful monster.

Just when I think my stomach is empty, it rolls again. I throw up until I taste bile.

I can't just kill Darius and Percy. Not now. Not while my sister is here somewhere. It's too risky. I won't risk her life like Papa risked ours.

I flush the toilet and wipe my mouth with a towel. When I come out of the bathroom, the image of my father is standing at the foot of my bed, waiting for me.

"You lied to me," I accuse.

Papa looks to the ground and then to me with tear-filled eyes. He raises his hands in apology and shakes his head.

"You believed in this shit!" I cry, raising to my knees. "The entire time! You got your wife and daughters killed! And, for what? For this?"

His shoulders fall.

"You are just a product of my imagination. A coping mechanism. I know this. But I'm glad for some reason my brain decided to allow me to see you but not hear you today because there's nothing you could say that I want to hear." I laugh, bitterly. "I've mourned for you. I've made myself sick, thinking about the night I lost you. I went along with everything you asked me to do for all of these years, and for what? So, you could parade your picture-perfect *white* family around to these pieces of shit?" I shake my head. "You know, I used to think you were the smartest man in the whole world." Tears prick at the backs of my eyes, but I refuse to cry for him. I refuse to shed one more tear for the man responsible for the death of my mother and sisters. "I thought you weren't emotional or feeling or lovey-dovey with us because you were the intelligent type. The kind that didn't think of those kinds of things, that it didn't come naturally to you. But, I know now it's because you were a hateful person, and you just didn't have it in you to show love. You were everything to me growing up, and now? Now, you're nothing. You infected so many people with the idea of hate, and they spread it to so many more, leaving lives and people broken and lost all because they caught your plague." I walk up to the ghostly image of him, frozen in place. I point a finger through his chest. "You are not my Papa anymore. You never were."

I storm right through his image to the door. "Now, if you'll excuse me, I'm going to find Mindy and get the fuck out of this hell you created, while you can disappear, and go back to the hell you belong in."

જ

THE HUMAN SENSE OF SMELL IS CLOSELY LINKED WITH memory, more so than any of our other senses. The smell of jasmine conjures long ago memories of my mother's perfume, the expensive one she only wore once a year on Christmas or her birthday. The smell of the salt in the air or sunscreen always reminds me of our family summers here in Logan's Beach and hours in the sun with my sisters. I can still hear them squealing as they splash one another in the water, the sound of the beach ball being volleyed back and forth into the air. The sound of the seagulls fighting for scraps of bread that Mallory always fed to them even though my father warned her not to. But, not all smells conjure good memories.

The compound of The Fourth Reich, the headquarters of hate, is located in the middle of an overgrown, wooded lot on the edge of town. It's the smell of pine trees, a thick, sappy odor that sticks to the inside of your nose. That smell used to remind me of this place every time I got a whiff of floor cleaner or a car air freshener. The memories were neither good nor bad, just research. And now that I know the truth, the scent is downright nauseating, each crunch of my foot-steps over the pine needles, infuriating.

Half of the uneven grounds are dry while another part closer to the compound is flooded, courtesy of the very recent Hurricane Polly.

The building itself is an old elementary school that closed when the new one, a combination of both elementary and middle schools opened up on the other side of town. The outbuildings consist of trailers in the back of the property that were formally portable classrooms used for student overflow. Now, they house the occasional visitor or the Reich member who partied too hard to make the trip home.

One of them contains my sister.

When I arrive at the trailers, I quietly pass under the trailer that belongs to Percy. I keep myself as close to the siding as possible, side-stepping under the windows. I am clear of the trailer by a single step when the door swings open. A brunette steps out wearing a short, leather skirt and black fishnet top over a magenta bra. She's holding a silver case-style purse under her arm. She looks at me for a second, appraising me. I hold my breath, waiting for her to shout something back to Percy, alerting him of my presence. But all she does is shoot me a bored look, obviously deciding that I'm not worth her time. She shuts the door quietly and makes her way down the steps through the courtyard, disappearing around the main building.

I exhale and try to catch my breath, grateful she didn't say anything or draw attention to my presence.

The portables are up on cement blocks, making it hard to see through any of the windows. I locate a discarded block laying on its side next to one of the trailers and try to lift it. It's much heavier than I thought, so I settle on having to drag it through the thick mud. It takes a few minutes, but I finally manage to position it under one of the back windows out of view from any potential prying eyes.

I step up and peer inside, cupping my hands around my eyes. There's a sheer curtain that veils my view but doesn't obstruct it.

Nothing.

It's absent of people but full of crap. Mattresses, desks stacked on top of one another, and cases of liquor take up every inch of room. Storage.

Shit. On to the next one. I drag the cement block to the next trailer, and by the time I get there, my arm is burning, and even though the sun has barely lit the sky, I'm sweating profusely. There's nothing in this one either. I search two more trailers. One houses a sleeping Hoppy on a tiny twin mattress; the other is completely empty.

On my fifth attempt, I peer into the window and spot a small blanket-covered being curled up on the tiny bed.

My heartbeat quickens. "Mindy," I whisper. I leap off the block and quietly search the perimeter around the trailer for any sign of a guard or any waking members of the Reich.

Nothing.

I tip-toe up the wooden steps leading to the door. It's locked. Not just locked, but chained from one side to the other with a metal bar screwed in on both sides.

Shit.

I drag another block to the window and set it on top of the other one. Thankfully, it's not locked, but it is stuck. I remove Pike's knife from my rain boot and use it to pry open the window, freeing it from the layers of paint coating the weather-stripping underneath.

When I think I've done enough to cause some movement, I give it another try. I practically cheer when it creaks open enough for me to crawl inside. Once I find footing on what I realize was the cage that was previously housing my sister, I peer out again to make sure the coast is clear. There's a small deer grazing at the corner of the field behind the compound, but as far as life outside the window goes, that's it.

I've got to get Mindy out of here before Percy decides her life isn't worth the trouble she might bring to the Reich. I have no idea what she knows or what she doesn't know. She hasn't spoken yet but it doesn't mean that she can't. And if they get her to talk, or worse, force her to talk, the possibility of her knowing that they are the ones responsible for our family's deaths is pretty high, especially considering that they're the ones who shoved her in a fucking cage.

Way to gain her trust, morons.

"I'll explain later, Mindy, but we have to go. Now." I say. I'm about to leap down from the cage when two strong hands grab my shoulders, tugging me back through the window.

My tailbone vibrates as I hit the ground. Hard. I'm dazed and dizzy as the image of a large man standing over me comes into focus.

A large, angry man. One with a Fourth Reich tattoo pulsing against his pale neck.

Percy.

"You're gonna get yourself fucking killed poking around back here," he mutters. "What the fuck are you doing out here anyway?"

I sit upright and try to stand, but stumble and fall down again, unable to catch my balance and unable to put too much pressure on my injured leg. I finally manage to get to my feet, but by the time I'm upright, Percy has already nailed a board over the window. I don't hear anything from within, and I realize the mattresses lining the walls are there for a reason.

A sound buffer.

"What are you doing?" I cry, desperate to get back inside to my sister.

Percy doesn't answer. He tucks the hammer into his back pocket and storms over to me with his eyebrows knitted together in a deep frown. He grabs me by the arm and drags me away from the trailer.

"Why is she in there? Why can't I see her?" I demand to know.

"Be quiet," he hisses. "Or you'll wake the whole damn fucking place up. I told you, you shouldn't be here." He peers around my head and then behind him, checking for onlookers. There aren't any. "And stop asking so many fucking questions."

"But I saw her, and I couldn't help myself. Put yourself in my shoes." I try to remember the part I'm playing and do my best to center myself back into the role of Reich member. Someone who isn't Percy's enemy, but on his side. "I know she's a gift. Thank you."

"How the fuck did you know that?" he asks, gripping my arm tighter.

I shrug. "Small compound. People talk. Is she okay?"

"Still figuring that out. Come on." Percy tugs me to the front of the trailer where Hoppy is now outside, shirtless, stretching and yawning. He spots us and smiles.

"Morning, kids," he greets, scratching a dark hairy nipple.

Percy stops but doesn't loosen his grip on my arm. "Hey, Hop, put a fucking shirt on, will ya?" His tone is casual and very different from the seething angry one he's just used with me.

He's acting. But why?

Hoppy rubs his big belly. "Fuck you, Perc. You're just fucking jealous because there's more of me for the ladies to love." He glances from me to Percy. "Hey, what's got you two kids up so early?"

I expect Percy to tell him. To say something that would result in me being locked in a trailer of my own at the very least. Instead, he releases my elbow and wraps his arm around my shoulder, pulling me into him. "Oh, you know," Percy wags his eyebrows suggestively and bites his bottom lip.

Hoppy's smile brightens. "Ah, now I get it. You two aren't up early, you're doing the walk of shame. I know how you do, brother. Good to see you kids are taking this marriage thing seriously and finally getting it on the way God intended." Hoppy balls his fists and jerks his hips, humping the air. He laughs and turns back toward the trailer. "Still on to get that part for my truck around noon, P?" he calls back.

Percy guides us back toward the main building. "Only if you put on a fucking shirt first," he replies.

"Wait, you give the little lady her gift yet?" Hoppy asks.

Percy stops us again and looks over his shoulder. "Not yet, waiting for the right time. Thanks for ruining the fucking surprise."

"Oopsie," Hoppy sings.

Percy pinches my shoulder, indicating that I should play along. "You have a gift for me?" I ask him, with mock surprise. "You didn't tell me! What is it?"

"Patience," Percy answers, his eyes locked on mine. "It's not ready yet."

"Very good. Sorry for the fuck up. Carry on, children." Hoppy gives us a fat middle finger solute and steps back into his trailer while whistling a Disney song from...if I'm not mistaken, *Frozen*?

Percy takes me by the elbow once more, reconsidering the main building, he pulls me inside his trailer, shutting the door behind us and locking it.

Unlike the other trailers I've searched, Percy's is clutter free. The sparse decorations consist of a swastika flag hanging above his unmade twin bed, a Fourth Reich medal hanging over a crooked desk with a framed picture of his deceased mother on top.

"What the fuck is going on, Percy?" I stomp my foot on the floor, ready to unleash hell and get answers at any cost. "Why didn't you tell Hoppy that I know about the gift? Why can't I see her?"

"I know you've got a big fucking heart, Mickey, but you're asking a lot of questions you shouldn't be asking," he replies, nostrils flaring. "Stop poking around. I fucking mean it." He paces the small room. "She's safe in there. I promise. She shouldn't even be here. YOU shouldn't even be here." He steps to the window and pushes aside the curtain, checking left and right before letting it fall back into place. "None of this shit was my idea."

His chin drops to his chest.

"Wait, what are you talking about? Why shouldn't we be here? What wasn't your idea?" Right now, I would rather have the usual straight-up angry and hateful version of Percy. At least I know how that one worked. This quieter secretive version of him is one I've never seen before. I'm not prepared to handle it, and in my world, unforeseen variables are the most surprising, but can also be the most terrifying.

"It was a mistake for you to come back here, Mickey. Especially 'cause that gunshot in your leg is obviously self-inflicted. And, since you ain't dead, I know it wasn't all trouble over at Pike's place." He turns to face me. "You should have just fucking stayed there."

"What?" I ask, unable to hide the shakiness in my question and surprised at how much I've underestimated Percy's skill for observation. "Why would I do that?"

"Look," Percy says, his eyes meeting mine. "I'm a fucking asshole, but I don't care that you were with Pike. I know this wedding thing is something our dads pushed on us. It's not exactly like we're in love. I only care that you came back. You shouldn't have fucking come back. I'm not always honest, but believe me when I say that I've always liked you Mickey. Even when we were kids. I didn't know how to show it, but you were always nice to me even when I wasn't nice to be around. Even when I wasn't nice to myself. That's always stuck with me."

"I—"

"Never liked me at all and wished I was still locked up?" he finishes for me.

He's not wrong. He also doesn't wait for a reply because he already knows the answer, along with a lot of other things I didn't think he knew anything about.

"I'm not trying to hurt you or…"

"Mindy," I answer, finally saying her name aloud.

"The name. Your sister. *Mindy.*" he says with a smile that I want to rip off his face. He has my sister locked in a trailer and doesn't even know her name or which of my sisters he has.

I straighten my shoulders. "Yes, that's her name," I reply, "*Mindy.*" It feels good to same her name, even if it's to one of the men holding her hostage.

"Alright, well, it was Darius's idea to give her to you as a wedding gift or some shit. She wasn't in good shape when he brought her here."

"What happened to her? Where has she been all this time?"

"I'm not sure really. But Darius doesn't want me to give her to you if she's not in good shape."

"You mean he wants you to *kill* her," I accuse.

"Yeah, that's what I mean. Listen, I'm a monster, but even that's out of my fucking realm. I think she'll pull through just fine. But, I'm going to need you to trust me and stay away. You can go back to swearing under your breath and giving me fake smiles later. Right now, just promise me. No more looking around, because trust me, you're not going to like what you find." He sighs and mutters something barely audible. Something that sounds a lot like, *I know I didn't.*

"I understand what you're trying to tell me," I reply, "but you're not telling me why."

"You're smart, Mickey. Stay that way. Use that big brain of yours. Keep your head down. You don't have to like me. You just have to trust me enough to let me do my thing and keep you alive."

"Mindy, too?" I ask.

He pauses. "Mindy, too. Do we have an understanding?"

I stand from the bed and approach Percy. "We do, but promise me that when the time comes, you'll help me get her out of here," I say. "Because you're right. She shouldn't be here."

"I can promise that I'll try," he says, holding out his hand.

I look at his hand, but I don't take it. "That's not good enough."

He rolls his eyes and extends his hand again. "I promise that I'll try to get her out of here before the wedding. Mindy. I'll try to get *Mindy* out of here before the wedding."

The wedding. Our wedding.

It's an ice-cold reminder that I'm working on a timeline.

The wedding is in two weeks. That's all the time I have to get my sister out of this place before I have to face The Reich and make vows to Percy that I never intend to keep, and this complicated storyline becomes even more tragic.

The old school bell rings, indicating the beginning of the Reich's weekly meeting.

"I have so many questions," I tell him.

He frowns and waits for the bell to stop ringing. "I'll never be able to give you most of the answers you want, but just trust me. Please. Just this once."

I'm not sure if he's making me a promise or a threat, but regardless, there's a lot more going on in this place and with Percy than I've suspected. He's suddenly become a more complicated character in this terrible story. I'm more than a little curious to find out what motivations are behind his new role.

Also, how can I promise to keep away from Mindy when I've just found her again? When, regardless of what he says, she could still be in danger?

"Stop." Percy opens the door. "Don't even think what you're thinking, Mickey."

I cross my arms stubbornly over my chest. "You don't know what I'm thinking."

His smile is sad. "I do. It's written all over your face...and it's gonna fucking get you killed."

4

PIKE

"Machine Head" by Bush blares through my truck speakers, fueling me forward. I lower it as I turn down a back road that runs parallel to the one that houses the compound of The Fourth Reich. I keep my headlights on until I find the path I need to turn onto that will take me through the field. I flip the lights off as my truck tires leave the pavement. I bump along the path, then kill the engine when I've gotten as far as I can unnoticed. I keep the key in the ignition, so the music keeps playing, but lower it even more. I don't need to. It's not like they'd be able to hear the music from my truck over the screaming and scratching blaring through their speakers that punches at my chest with every beat.

It's garbage music, but it fits the Reich perfectly.

Because just like them, it has no rhythm, no rhyming, and no fucking reason.

It's like they're all a bunch of fucking kids rebelling against their parents.

I'm all about being the rebel, but there's a difference

between fighting against a true enemy and fighting against one you gotta create in order to win.

These bitches are so weak, they pick battles with people that don't even know there's a war.

It's fucking laughable. What's next, picking a fight with grandma over what kind of tea she serves? It's ridiculous and just as pointless.

I'm not the smartest man in the world, but even I can see there's no fucking logic behind their shit. Just a bunch of misguided fucking kids finding the wrong purpose. Screaming for attention, trying to be heard over all the fucking noise.

The smell from the bonfire permeates the air. A scent I'm naming *hickory, hicks, and hate.*

I watch the crowd for a while, and just when I think I'm not going to see her, there she is. Mickey appears, wandering around the party, staying mostly on the outside of the crowd.

My chest tightens, and my cock leaps with fucking delight.

Talk about no logic. My dick doesn't seem to have any.

"Down boy, she could be a bad girl," I mutter.

It doesn't listen.

"Not that kind of bad girl," I grumble, white-knuckling the steering wheel.

Although, the image of tying her to my bed right now, naked and spread before me, punishing her, isn't exactly an unwelcome one.

She's wearing a denim skirt and a black tank top, showing off the brand on her shoulder she spent the entire time at my place trying to hide. Not anymore. Now, it's proudly on display. A mark that proves to the Reich that she's one of them.

It makes my stomach turn to think of her as one of them. As sick as the thought is, and as probable as it is, I don't want to believe it's true. All that time in the alley caring for fucking cats? It gives me hope that she can't possibly hold the kind of hate in her heart needed to associate with these fucks.

But that's why I'm here. To find out the truth.

I'll give her fucking credit though. Whatever side she's manipulating, she's good at it. There's no doubt about that. It's almost funny how you can make someone believe something that they want to see. And also to her credit, Mickey is fucking brave. The brand. The way she stood up to me when I had her locked up in my fucking garage? She's capable of anything, and it both terrifies me and turns me the fuck on.

I see Percy, chugging a beer with a big, burly guy who then crushes the can against his forehead as Mickey watches. The big guy gives a victorious yell, then wobbles from foot to foot, either because of the impact of the can or drunkenness. Possibly a little of both.

I roll my eyes as Percy lifts another one, and they repeat the process to the roaring cheers of the other morons eager to gain the approval of their future almighty leader.

Seriously, they should make a documentary about these people. If nothing else, it would be good for a laugh.

Shit, I'm not the smartest man, but these motherfuckers make me feel like I've gained a few IQ points in the few minutes I've been watching them.

The big guy spins in a circle, victoriously accepting the applause for his drunken idiocy. Percy claps and slaps the guy on the back. I can't help but think of how easy it would be right now.

It would only take one call to Sniper. He's in Bear's crew and ex-military. For a small fee or hell, probably just a six pack or the fun of it, I could have him pick these mother-fuckers off one by one. Pink mist everywhere.

No more Fourth Reich.

But that can wait, because right now I'm here for a reason, and right now, that reason is bending over to pick up the discarded beer cans Percy and his buddy just tossed to the ground. I catch a full glimpse of her rounded backside filling out her jean skirt. My cock twitches again. "It's not that kind of confrontation," I remind him out loud because I'm a crazy person now who talks to his cock. And partly because I wish it was that kind of confrontation.

Mickey looks around, then slowly makes her way into the dark toward the back of the building where not a single light shines through any of the windows.

Whatever kind of confrontation it is, it's happening now.

Tonight will decide Mickey's fate.

And mine.

MICKEY

PROMISES ARE THE SWEETEST KIND OF LIES. ALSO, THEY mean nothing spoken from a place of desperation, and that so happens to be exactly the place I find myself in. Lost in a void of desperation. Consumed with only the thoughts and desire to get to Mindy. All while playing the devoted fiancé to the future leader of The Reich at yet another shit-show of a party celebrating what, I'm not exactly sure. I never am.

Sneaking away from the party isn't easy. I wait for forever for what feels like the perfect moment when I think I won't be missed. I find that moment between the *forehead beer crushing* competition and the *how fast can you run through the bonfire without burning to death* dare.

Slowly, I back away from the crowd until I'm fully enveloped in the shadows of the side of the building. Once I know I can't be seen, I turn and run at full speed. When I reach the lighted courtyard, I slow my pace. I come across a couple walking back into the main building. We exchange polite greetings and I try not to breathe too heavily and show my exertion. The second they're gone from view, I race to the trailer, and I throw open the door.

Only, it's empty. At least, it's empty of Mindy. All that remains are the mattresses and other crap that were there before. Even the cage that was under the window is now gone.

I shut the door quietly and resume my search. I try and tell myself that it will be okay. That Percy promised to protect her.

But promises are the sweetest lies. You just thought that yourself.

Shit.

Casually, I attempt to make my search look like a meandering stroll, whistling and gazing up at the stars occasionally. While on the inside I'm yelling at myself to run from door to door and tear them off the hinges.

After what feels like hours, I've covered the entire compound, checking open doors and peering through windows with no luck at all.

The bass of the party shakes the walls of the hall as I get closer to the party. The bonfire light shines through the archway leading out into the courtyard. I stop, unable to propel myself any further. I can't go back there. I just can't.

I take a step back and then turn, running into the girl's bathroom. I check the stalls for feet and find none. I lock the door behind me and rest my back against it, sliding to the floor.

My thoughts shift from my sister to Pike and how I wish he was here right now. How I wish I could lose myself in his arms when it all gets too much like I did when I was with him.

I wonder if he'll ever forgive me for leaving like I did or if he even cares that I left?

Probably the latter, considering I brought him nothing but trouble while I was there, but even that thought feels wrong as I remember how caring he was. How he touched my leg and held my hand as I told him and Nine the truth about my father, the truth about why I was involved with the Reich in the first place.

I rest my forehead on my knees, lost in my own thoughts and an overwhelming sadness.

A loud stomp echoes in the small bathroom, and my head shoots up to find the very source of my thoughts standing above me.

Pike.

"You," I breath, clamoring to my feet.

"Expecting someone else?" Pike drawls, eyes raking over my body. There's heat in his eyes along with something else. It's pain. The same pain I saw reflected when I told him I had him figured out in his pawn shop.

"No, but...why are you here?" I ask, smoothing down my skirt and feeling just as nervous as I did when he approached me for the first time in his garage. He has the same dark warning in his eyes that he had that night. An icy tremor breaks out at the base of my spine, causing my entire body to shiver.

"I have a question for you." Pike stalks forward, closing the space between us. His masculine scent along with his nearness wraps around me. "Do you know what it's really like to kill someone? To have blood on your hands? And I'm not talking about the physical act of taking someone's life. I'm talking about what it does to you. What you'll feel after. It's not as easy as you think. It's not something you can't undo, and it may not be something you can come back from."

Suddenly, I go from happy he's here to enraged. "Why? Because my mind has broken before, and you think it will break again? You don't think I've thought of that? That I know the risks?"

He cages me in, backing me up to the one of the three sinks. "I don't want you to go to a place you'll never come back from. It's selfish, but I don't want to lose you. I can't."

"I...have to do this," I say, my voice shaky.

His nostrils flare. "What exactly is this grand plan of yours, Mic? Because whatever you do, it won't bring them back, and it will probably wind up getting you killed."

"It doesn't matter if I die or not," I try to explain.

"It matters to me," Pike seethes.

I suck in a breath. "Why?"

He looks me over and frowns. "I'm not sure, but it does. It matters more than anything."

I shake my head. "No. I don't. You can't—"

He wraps a strong hand around my wrist.

"No!" I wrench out of his grasp. "People who care about me end up getting hurt or killed. So you see, you can't care about me."

He grabs me and pushes me back against the sink. He holds my jaw, forcing me to look into his eyes. "The only person who can hurt me right now, is you. It's your fucking move, Mic. Make sure you make the right one."

"How?" I ask, feeling a stabbing sensation over and over again within my chest. "What choice do I have?"

He lowers his face until his lips are hovering over mine. "I'll tell you…after."

"After what?" I ask, but no sooner do the words leave my mouth that his lips are on mine. Devouring me along with any thoughts I had about anything else.

There's only me and Pike.

It feels right. More so than anything has over the past few days.

Pike looks and smells like a woman's version of a wet dream. Or maybe, that's just my reaction to him, although that sounds ridiculous even as I think it because there's no woman alive that wouldn't be affected by his strong shoulders, his wide gate, the casual unaffected hard stare in his blazing eyes. Hormone-driven response or not, I've never wanted anything more in my life than I want to feel Pike's hands on me, the weight of his naked body on mine, the warmth of his skin wrapping around me as he thrusts his hot cock inside of me.

My cheeks burn with redness, and suddenly, the humid night air is too much to bear. I'm a prisoner in my own clothes.

I yearn for Pike to free me from captivity. To feel him again. Against me. Inside of me.

"I love this," he says, running his knuckles over my cheek, and I know he's talking about my blushing because he's said as much before. I lean into his touch and look up at him with parted lips. "I want to see you blush everywhere."

His nostrils flare as he drops to his knees and parts my thighs with his hands. He pushes my panties to the side, burying his nose between my folds, inhaling deeply. I close my legs out of sheer embarrassment, but he shakes his head. "You can't fucking hide from me," he growls against my clit. The stubble on his face causes a friction that sends the pulsing sensation in my core into overdrive, tightening, needing, feeling all too empty. Pike digs his fingers into my thighs, keeping them spread apart. "Don't you fucking dare to try and keep me from what's mine." He swipes his tongue over my clit and grazes his teeth over the sensitive nub. I buck, my back flying off the sink as a blinding jolt of pleasure shocks me like I've been struck by lightning.

Pike holds me down, pressing on my lower stomach, keeping me pressed against the sink. "Where do you think you're going?" He chuckles, repeating the lick with very much the same, if not a stronger, response from me. He, then, opens his mouth, licking and sucking on my clit, gently at first, like he's kissing my lips, passionately, furiously before circling his tongue faster and faster in a rhythm that has me turning my head from one side to the other on the mattress, unsure of what to do while my body is being assaulted with the most extreme pleasure in existence.

He grabs my ankles and pushes them up, bringing my knees to my chest and parting my legs even wider. His tongue moves faster. He swirls and sucks, inserting a finger and lightly biting on my clit at the same time. The tightness in my lower stomach releases into an atomic bomb of an orgasm that explodes with such ferocity that my muscles spasm as they contract, sending me into a blinding wave of pleasure that I'm sure I'll drown in.

He stands, leaving me breathless and spread before him. I feel the loss of his touch while burning for more.

"Don't worry. I ain't fuckin' going nowhere," he assures me, knowing exactly what I want. What I need. "I ain't done with you yet."

He reaches behind my neck and lifts my head up to kiss me, his tongue exploring my greedy mouth. I can taste myself on his tongue. "You taste so fucking good. Everywhere," he says against my lips, never breaking the kiss. I reach up and thread my fingers through his hair, pulling him closer. My hard nipples graze his chest, sending an aftershock of rippling pleasure through my entire body. "You want more, Mic?"

I can only nod against his mouth, breathing heavily.

"You want it all?" he asks, sounding raspy and rough as if he's about to lose control.

"Yes," I manage to say, reaching for the hem of his shirt and pulling it over his head. I wrap my legs around his waist again and dig my heels into his ass, urging him on.

He hisses. "Fuck, Mic, I wish I could take my time with you."

"There's no time. I want you to fuck me," I hear myself say, although it doesn't even sound like me. My need for Pike has become a full body possession of lust and want.

Pike spins me around and bends me over the sink. I grip the edge to prevent falling face-first against the porcelain. I glance up at him through the mirror to where he's standing behind me, appraising my body with fierce heat in his fiery eyes. He molds his body against mine. I close my eyes at the sensation I've been dreaming about since the last time I saw him. I relish in his scent, his heat.

"Open your eyes, Mic," he orders. "I want you to see this. To see us," he demands, unbuckling his jeans and pushing down on his boxers.

My only response is a whimper. I have no words.

Only need.

As ordered, I open my eyes.

Pike grazes the back of my neck with his lips. "I want to see your reaction in the mirror as you take my cock. I want you to see mine as I give it to you. I'm not just going to fuck you. This is a message. One I want you to receive loud and fucking clear so that there will be no more misunderstandings between us." He reaches between my legs under my skirt, cupping my pussy over my damp panties.

I push back into him with a needy groan. He holds me in place, pushing my panties down my legs before resuming his touch, this time against bare and soaking wet flesh.

He groans when he feels what's waiting for him. "*This* belongs to me." He wraps an arm around my shoulder, closing a hand over my throat, biting at my earlobe. His next words are both a statement and a warning, delivered while the shaft of his thick cock presses against the cleft of my ass. "You. Belong. To. Me."

He pulls back briefly, then enters me with no warning, and with such force, that I'm dizzy as he stretches me open, filling me completely. He doesn't pause before beginning an all-out assault on my pussy.

"Holy shit," he rasps, echoing my thoughts.

I grip the sink for support as Pike relentlessly fucks me from behind, pushing and pulling on my waist as he pounds into me. My body convulses every time his hips connect with the flesh of my ass.

"Are you looking, Mic?" he asks, teasing his lips against my cheek. He holds my jaw and turns my face until his harsh kisses slant across my lips, as hard and furious as he's fucking me. I'm breathless when he releases me. "Are you?" he repeats, releasing my face.

My only answer is to push back my hips.

He hisses at the contact and tugs my hair, stinging my scalp. It burns, but his reaction is the reason why I don't hesitate to do it again. "Mic," he warns, wrapping my hair around his hand. "Look," he orders, using his grip on my hair to direct my head so that I have no choice but to look.

In the mirror, I see Pike, glistening with sweat, looking very much like an angel carrying out the devil's work. I'm suddenly very grateful I have a photographic memory because this image is one I'll recall often, and for the rest of my life. A flush of wetness escapes my body, drenching his cock with appreciation. "Fuck," he swears. "I take it that you like what you see?"

I manage to nod, pulling against his grip on my hair, my eyes watering as the stinging of my scalp becomes more of a burning.

Pike releases my hair. My head falls forward, but I don't dare drop my gaze. He told me to look, and that's precisely what I plan to do.

A devilish smirk plays on his lips as he digs his fingernails into my ass. He looks down and runs his hands over my flesh, admiring the marks he's undoubtedly leaving in his wake. The muscles in his arms and chest are taut, straining against his tattooed skin in his effort to both fuck me and break me. Beneath his furrowed brows, there's a crazed look in his eyes that's both frightening and thrilling.

I push back against his thrust once more, and this time, he growls. It's a sound so low and primal I can feel it deep within my trembling body.

"You trying to push me over the edge?" he rasps, staring at my reflection with heavily hooded eyes.

I can't help myself, and maybe, I am trying to push him over the edge.

I wink.

Pike makes a sound similar to that of a starved animal. He grabs my jaw and turns my head sideways, forcing my cheek flat against the cold porcelain. Two of his thick fingers open my lips, penetrating my mouth. His thrusts become more determined, more desperate as if he's trying to fuck the insolence out of me.

Fat chance.

I'm not sure if I act out of instinct, or if it's just my need to prove to him that he's not the only one in charge, or if I really do want to push him over the edge and see what happens, but it's certainly not out of sanity that I choose to bite down on his fingers.

Hard.

So hard, I taste his coppery blood on my tongue.

Feeling victorious, I grin around his bloody fingers, keeping my teeth buried in his flesh.

"You're going to fucking kill me," Pike moans, but he doesn't pull his fingers from my mouth. He doesn't pull away at all. If anything, the bite causes him to become more unhinged, fueling his already maddening pace, smashing my breasts against the rattling sink—dust from where the sink and wall meet falls to the ground.

Pike pushes down on my shoulders and lifts my hips so that I'm standing on the balls of my feet, legs spread as wide as they can go, making myself as open to him as I can possibly be. He drives into me with a force that's not just going to break the wall but likely break me in half. I grip the side of the sink with both hands, holding on with all of my strength. I meet his every thrust with a push of my own, determined to give it as good as I can take it as my muscles strain, and my body relishes in the pleasure of it all.

The power.

Pike finally pulls his fingers from my mouth. Blood drips from the corner of my lips. I try and catch my breath, but there are no breaks. There's just me and Pike and this dangerous thing between us that has us pulling and pushing against each other as if possessed by demons.

Or maybe, we *are* the demons.

Possessed or not, my legs shake. My knees grow weak. To keep from falling, I lift one arm and press my hand against the mirror. My lower stomach clenches and begins to spasm, and I'm not sure how much longer I can hold this position. I begin to slip, but push up with my feet onto my toes, pressing harder against the mirror. On my other hand, my knuckles are white as I tighten my grip on the edge of the sink, desperate to stay upright. Desperate to feel all of this. To feel *him.*

"Fuck, Mic," Pike moans, his cock thickening inside me, pulsing against my inner walls. His thighs behind to shake against the back of my legs. I'm still looking in the mirror, but my vision blurs as my body tightens around his cock. All I see is a now fuzzy image of two bodies looking to both pleasure and punish the other.

I adjust my hand as my feet again threaten to slip, clawing at the mirror, wishing it wasn't so damn smooth.

"You better be fucking watching," Pike grates through gritted teeth. I blink rapidly and focus on the chording of Pike's neck as my vision clears.

"Pike!" I cry as a wave of pleasure threatens to burst within me. My entire body begins to tremble with my impending orgasm, and if this is only a preview, I'm elated and fucking terrified of what's to come.

The room smells like sweat and sex. The sounds of the slapping of skin on skin fill the small room, along with our grunts and groans.

I use everything I have to push back against Pike, taking what I want, no, what I *need.*

"Yes," he rasps. 'That's it. Mic. That's my fucking girl. Give me all you got."

Releasing my grip on the sink, I use both hands to push against the mirror, giving him what he's asking for.

It's too much. The mirror cracks under the added pressure, spider-webbing around my fingers and slicing into my skin.

My body tightens around Pike's cock, gripping him from the inside.

Pike's rhythm becomes erratic and wild. He wraps his arms around my waist, holding me tightly in place against his body.

Blood drips from my fingers, painting our reflections red.

We don't stop fucking.

Pike grips my jaw again, placing his chin on my shoulder, forcing me to watch our distorted bloody images in the spider-webbed glass that has broken us into two pieces. Pike in one and me in the other.

We don't stop fucking.

Glass begins to fall, dropping into the sink and onto our bodies, pricking at our skin.

We fuck harder.

Pike's name tears from my lips as I reach the edge, glass raining down all around us.

We fuck even harder.

The piece with my image falls.

Pike groans out my name on a strangled cry that pushes me into a kind of pleasure that's both painful and brutal and soothing and bliss all at the same time.

"Mic," he breathes, as I'm still feeling the bliss tear through my body. He rests his head on my shoulder.

The last piece, the one with his reflection, falls into the sink.

The mirror is now completely shattered.

And so are we.

෴

I'M STILL DAZED FROM WHAT JUST HAPPENED WHEN PIKE grabs my face in his hands and stares deeply into my eyes. "Mic, let me help you. I won't stand in your way, but I'll help you get your revenge. Come with me now, and we will figure this shit out together."

I shake my head and think of my sister. I can't leave her, not now. I don't even know where she is. "No. You can't...I can't." Tears well up in my eyes. "I..." I start, wanting to explain further, but not being able to find the words. What am I trying to say? I love you please understand? I can't say anything because any words that leave my lips won't come out right. I'm not good with the ones that involve feelings, and right now, I'm feeling so much. "I want to, but I can't leave because—"

The door handle jiggles followed by three hard thumps. "Who is in there? Mickey, is that you?"

"Come with me," Pike says again, pulling up his pants. "Please, Mic. Come on." He extends his hand, and all I can think about is that if I take it, my sister is as good as dead.

"Mickey?" the voice asks again.

A tear spills down my cheek. "I just can't."

Pike stares at me, and I can see the hurt in his eyes until, suddenly, it's gone and replaced with something else. I know, in this moment, I've said the wrong thing. Something I can't take back. The shift in him feels permanent. A new reality of what's to come, and I can feel the intensity of whatever he's just decided in my very bones. "For what it's worth, I wanted this. I wanted you. What happens now, you should know, it's on you."

He begins to lift himself up to the window, and I charge him, yanking him down by his shirt. I hold his face in my hands, stand up on my tip-toes, and kiss him with everything I have. It's too short and brief, and when I pull away, I only have a second to glimpse the look in his eyes. A look that says goodbye because something tells me that after what he's just said, this is it for us.

The end.

"Mickey! Why is this shit locked!" Percy calls out.

Pike gives me one last confused, burning look, then leaps out the window, shutting it behind him. I straighten myself in the mirror and hope that the properly fucked look I'm sporting can also pass as drunk and disheveled.

I unlock the door, and Percy practically falls into the bathroom. He walks in and checks each of the stalls before noticing the broken mirror and the blood. "What the fuck happened?" Percy asks.

"I drank too much. I came in here to puke and fell right into the mirror," I lie, swaying a little for emphasis.

Percy looks at the mirror again, and I think he's about to call me out on the impossibility of falling into a mirror above the sink without taking a running leap at it, but his stance softens, and he seems to believe me because his face turns from surprise to concern. "Come with me. Let's get that hand bandaged up for you."

I wrap some toilet paper around my hand and shake my head. "I've got it. I have a first aid kit in my room."

"You sure?" he asks.

I nod. "Percy, where's Mindy?" I ask, holding a piece of toilet paper over my hand, blood soaking through the white tissue instantly.

"I told you not to go poking around." He glances at my bleeding hand again. "She's safe, Mickey. Go patch yourself up."

Feeling defeated and used and sated all at the same time, I barrel past Percy through the main doors and up the stairs toward my room, leaving a bloody trail in my wake…and so much more.

ᘓ

HOURS LATER, I'M IN MY SMALL BED, FEELING THE BEAT OF the music shaking the walls of my small room from the party still raging below. The moonlight shines through the window and casts light on my face.

I never cried when my family died. Not real tears. They were for show for the benefit of Darius and my commitment to my act about not knowing he was the one responsible for their demise. I didn't have time for real tears then, and I don't have time for them now.

My tears and my grief are my own, and I refuse to give them to him. The time to grieve isn't now. It's when this is all over. And I fear the grief on that day more than the killing that needs to be done by my own hands.

I've always been a loner. Even when I was living in a house with my sisters and my parents. I'd always find time to be by myself and my own thoughts. I crave and function well in solitude. That's what's gotten me through this. By myself. Making plans. Scheming. Calculating. Trusting no one. I'd spend hours in the middle of the night dreaming on how to bring my plans to fruition and now those dreams, although still there, have company. New dreams.

Of Pike.

Now that I know him, now that I have felt his body against mine, inside mine, now I know he exists in this world, my solitude has become stifling. The air is thick and hard to breathe. The air is hotter and more humid than usual. I don't just miss him. I crave him, body and soul. I find myself scratching at my own skin, trying to relieve an itch that isn't on the surface and can't be soothed by running my nails over my arms again and again until I draw blood.

Missing someone who is dead and never coming back doesn't go away but dulls over time as acceptance settles in. Missing someone who is alive is a pain that only grows with each tick of the clock.

I didn't cry when my family died. Not real tears. Just an act for Darius's sake to prove I didn't know what he'd done.

If I didn't cry then, I'm not going to cry now. Even though I feel like my insides are broken. Even though I can't breathe without feeling sharp pangs of regret. If only we were different people leading different lives. Maybe, I would be that summer tourist that catches his eye. Maybe, he'd be the bad boy who owned the pawn shop that I wouldn't be able to help but to swoon over.

But none of that matters now. Not my aching heart or my empty soul. I came back to the Fourth Reich to fulfill my revenge alone and now I stay because of my sister.

That look in his eyes before he left. The warning of his words. It was all so…final.

For a second, with Pike at his shop and in his bed, I was happy. I laugh at myself. What is happiness anyway but a mixture of chemical reactions inside the brain? A splash of dopamine, a smidge of serotonin, and a little oxytocin for flavor. It's a formula, not a feeling. The same effect can be achieved with a pill. It's an illusion.

But knowing that happiness is an illusion doesn't make my chest feel any less tight, or my throat any less dry, or my entire body feel less like it's being slowly lowered into a dark fucking hole never to come out again. I take a deep breath to steady myself.

I. WILL. NOT. CRY.

Pike is the only person I ever saw myself in. Which sounds fucking delusional because we are so different, opposite in almost every way, except where we are the same. Our determination, our pain, our loneliness, the way we try to fill the gaps in our lives. Him with things in his shop, me with my research and revenge.

We're both just filling a void. If it wasn't for my sister, I would have taken his hand and went with him. Revenge doesn't fill my heart the way Pike does. He's the key.

And I just changed the fucking locks.

5

PIKE

THERE'S NO SHITTIER feeling than knowing you have to kill someone whose pussy you can still taste on your lips.

Numb is all I want to feel, but every time I close my eyes, I imagine the look in Mickey's eyes...right before I end her life.

It's not a nightmare. It's the fucking future. Maybe, I was dumb enough to believe, to hope, that she'd come with me, and I wouldn't have to deal with the rest of this shit. A big part of me never thought she'd stay there, but she did. Again, she chose them.

Mic will be dead. Gone. Not of this fucking world.

It's as if all of my ribs have been broken.

Nobody can see the injury, but it's there, and it's very real.

My face twists in agony with each memory of her. I hold my hand to my chest, rubbing the skin as if it could somehow ease the ache beneath, but it does nothing to help because there is no cure for the kind of sickness I'm suffering from.

Drowning myself in whiskey is the closest I've found to relief, but only because I drink enough to render myself unconscious, but the second my eyes open, I reach for her. I think of her. I still smell her on my pillowcases. Even after washing them several times. I know her scent isn't there, but it's as if my mind wants to remind me that it was there once. To remember it.

To remember *her*.

Like I could ever fucking forget her.

I feel like I've been in a terrible car accident, and I'm bleeding internally.

I reach for the bottle of whiskey on my desk, only to find it frustratingly empty. I throw it across the room, and it shatters against the door just as it opens.

This feeling is temporary, I tell myself. It isn't real because the person you've lost isn't real. I'll be done wallowing soon, and when I do, if there is a god out there, may he have mercy on Mickey.

Because I sure as fuck won't.

Thorne looks at the shattered glass on the floor and rolls her eyes. "You done throwing yourself a pity party? Because we've got fucking work to do."

I groan. "You can run the pawn shop by yourself. Let's face it. You've been doing it for years anyway."

"True. But that's not the kind of business I'm talking about." She stands above me next to the bed and smacks a rolled-up newspaper onto my chest.

I shift to a sitting position. "Thanks, but I was born in a decade where my generation reads these things online." I slide the paper to the floor.

"Uhhhh." Thorne picks up the paper and unrolls it. She turns it upside down, and a note drops from between the pages.

Tonight. My studio. 8pm. -King

I read the words and rub my face in my hands. Fuck. He probably wants to discuss the raid of the compound. What night and what time Mickey is going to die. When I take my hands away, I see a foot tapping impatiently on the floor, reminding me of Thorne's presence. I look up to where she has her arms crossed over her chest and a hip jutted out with her lips pursed.

"Thank you," I say. Although he could have just sent a text to my burner phone. I guess he wants to be extra careful since digital trails can never truly be deleted. At least, that's what Nine's always harpin' on about. Besides, when you're planning a mass murder, it's always best to veer on the side of caution.

"Get your head out of your ass." Thorne leans over me and sniffs, then pinches her nose shut, fanning a hand in the air. "And for fuck's sake, take a shower, man."

It's true, I could use a shower, but in my drunken state last night, it was the last thing on my mind. Actually, in my drunken state, I'm not even sure how I got back to the pawn shop. The last thing I remember is drinking whiskey with Nine at his place. I sit up straight, stretching sore muscles and proceed to pretend to be looking for something under the stack of paper and receipts piled up on my desk. "Is that how you speak to your boss? Because that's what I am, in case you're having problems remembering," I snap. "Your *boss*."

I feel bad for snapping at her and for pulling the boss card because even though I met Thorne when she came to work here, I see her as a friend before an employee. It doesn't matter.

My words obviously don't have the impact I intended for them to have because Thorne looks to the ceiling and cackles. She stops suddenly and glares at me with hard accusing eyes.

She slaps both of her palms on the desk and leans in closer. "That's how I speak to my *boss* when he *was* the most fearless man I'd ever known and suddenly morphs into…" She waves her hand over me and grimaces. "Whatever this smelly, cowardly creature is."

Suddenly, rage boils within me, but what's making me most angry is that she's right. After all, avoiding the truth is the reason I'm drinking in the first place. I don't need her cold dose of reality, I need more fucking whiskey. I need more fucking time.

I slam my fist on the desk.

Thorne doesn't flinch. Because, well, Thorne *doesn't* flinch.

I speak through gritted teeth and point an accusing finger that should be pointed at myself, at her. "Don't you dare think you know what's fucking going on with me right now. You have no fucking idea." I turn to leave the room before I say something else to her that I'm going to regret later.

Thorne's words stop me in my tracks. "Oh, please, Pike. Do you really think you're the only one whose ever suffered from a broken heart before? You think you're the only one whose ever lost someone? Well, in case that's what you're thinking, allow me to clarify. You're not the first, and you won't be the last. You're not even the only person in this fucking room. So, do the world a favor, take a shower, and while you're at it, get the fuck over yourself."

I turn back around and cross my arms over my chest. Thorne's confession throwing a cold wet bucket of truth over my rage. "Who have you lost?" I ask, curiously. Thorne's never opened up to me like this, and as much as I consider her a trusted friend, there isn't a whole helluva lot I know about her past. Her family, which only reveals to me that I've been a shitty fucking friend because I never thought to ask.

She shrugs, and folds her hands together. "My mother and my brother. It was a long time ago," she says looking to the floor then to her nails. She quickly rebounds, straightening her shoulders and facing me once again.

"What happened?" I ask, taking a step toward her.

She sighs. "My mother died, and my brother, well, he's alive, and I never really knew him, but it doesn't make not getting the chance to grow up with him, to know him as a kid, feel like any less of a loss than my mother."

"Where is he now?" I ask, years too late.

"He's…" She shakes her head. "It doesn't matter. He's not exactly the family type."

My fists ball up. "Anyone who wouldn't want to be your family needs their heads removed from out of their asses more than I need my own."

She looks up and smirks. "You know, I couldn't have said it better myself."

I lift my arms to embrace Thorne, something I don't remember ever doing before, for her or anyone else, but it feels like the moment this sort of thing is done.

Thorne backs away and holds up a hand. "No. This isn't the time for that bullshit." She wrinkles her nose. "I'll take a rain check on that hug. Maybe, wait until after your shower. Or when the time is right. Or never." She releases her nose, and I drop my arms. "What it *is* time for is for you to go get your girl back without getting yourself killed."

I'm not sure what Thorne's not understanding. Mickey is gone. "Mickey left. She could have stayed, and she left. She chose to leave. She chose again to stay. I'm old school, but I'm not a caveman. I'm not going to drag her back here by her fucking hair. She chose *them*."

"I can't believe you can't see it!" Thorne suddenly shouts

with a stomp of her foot, her words echoing around the room like a thousand of her yelling at me. Or maybe, I'm not hungover, but still drunk, but at least, I'm only seeing one of her.

"See what?" I cry, pulling at my own hair in frustration. "There's nothing to see. She's fucking gone! It's over!" I look at my friend, and I can't understand what she's not understanding. "At least...she will be soon."

She purses her lips and steps close enough to me that I can smell her cherry shampoo and see the furry swimming in her eyes. "Greyson motherfucking Pike, you hear me, and you listen. Mickey left because she thought she had no other choice! She's there because she still thinks she has no other choice!" She spins in a circle, then drops her hands to her thighs, bending at the waist. "She knew that if you went after the Fourth Reich that you and the people you care about could die. She wasn't willing to take that chance because she's lost people and didn't want to lose you, too! She's doing this alone because she thinks she has to in order to protect you, you dumb fucking ox!"

"Why? Why would she do that?" I ask, still not understanding why leaving was somehow the better choice. "I'm still going after the Reich. I always was. She knows this. They set me up to look like I was stealing from King and..." I snap my fingers, "Oh, yeah, they fucking killed Gutter. Plus, I did hold her hostage, and there was that whole sensory torture thing. So, Thorne, tell me, why would she try and protect me? Why would she want to save *me*?"

My chest is heaving. My questions are rhetorical, but still, I wait for Thorne's answer, wondering what I missed that she sees so clearly.

Thorne stands straight and gently places her hands on my

chest, She looks up into my eyes with both sadness and compassion. More emotion than I've ever seen from her in all the years she's been around. "Mickey thinks she can take them down herself. She wants to so that you won't have to." She pauses and searches for something in my gaze. "Is it so hard for you to understand? To see what I see?" She frowns. "Or, do you just not think that you're worthy?" The way she asks leads me to believe that she's asking herself more than she's asking me.

I try to temper my frustration so that my anger doesn't blanket my words. "What am I not seeing? Tell me, Thorne. Help me to understand because it may be obvious to you, but it's not to me. I'm fucking lost here."

More lost than I've ever felt. More than when my mother left. More than when Gutter died.

Thorne holds my face in her hands, forcing me to look at her. "Pike, people protect the people they love. And Mickey?" A tear wells up in Thorne's eye and falls from the corner, trickling down her cheek. "She fucking loves you."

Her words punch at my chest like a steel fist. I recoil and feel behind me for the desk for support. I shake my head. "No, she can't. People who love you don't leave you."

"You think it's that cut and dry?" She chuckles. Love is complicated."

"Not in my experience. It's pretty easy. You love someone, and they leave. It means they don't love you back," I answer honestly.

She drops her hands. "What you mean is that your mother left you, and you think that means she didn't love you," Thorne accuses, accurately.

I search my memory for the time I told Thorne about my mother, but I come up blank. "How did you—"

She waves me off. "You were drunk slurring your way through your past one night and let it slip."

I'm a drunken confessor? Good to know. Maybe, whiskey isn't the best breakfast choice this morning.

Thorne nudges my shoulder "Did you ever stop and think she left because she loves you?"

"Mickey or my mom?" I ask.

"Both."

I answer honestly, "No."

"Well, you were wrong." She laughs. "So fucking wrong."

I say nothing because my mind is racing with this new idea. Mickey left, but not because she chose revenge over me, but because she *loves* me.

This changes everything.

"Someone finally crushed that stony heart of yours," Thorne says, perching on the desk next to me.

I take a deep, shaky breath and muster a half smile with my hand clenched over my chest. "Sure as fuck feels that way," I admit, and it's a surprising relief to admit a weakness I've always tried to hide from the rest of the world.

A new plan forms. One that will take every trustworthy person I know and a lot of fucking patience.

It's a plan that will see this shit through. And I'll kill every one of those fuckers if I have to, but I'm bringing Mickey back here with me where she belongs.

Home.

6

MICKEY

HORROR FILMS or zombie movies where people are hacked to bits and guts are strewn about like lawn decorations, are meant to provoke a reaction of disgust and fear within the viewer. But after a subject watches hundreds of those same kinds of violent movies, the same feelings they felt while watching the first are a mere flicker of what they were, becoming muted. The viewer now desensitized to the violent graphic images playing out in detail on the screen before them.

This doesn't just apply to movies. It applies to real life as well. When one hundred subjects living in high crime neighborhoods were given a survey about their level of fear, surprise, and adrenaline provoking circumstances, seventy percent of those subjects reported not even jumping in surprise or feeling fear-induced adrenaline rushes when hearing gunshots.

I grew up listening to the hate-filled words of The Fourth Reich every summer for two months. While I never ever thought what the Reich was preaching was right, I never remember a specific moment when I stepped outside of my scientific over-analytic mind and thought, "This is wrong." It was assumed. At least, I thought it was. I thought the fact that they were wrong was the one constant the entire psychological experiment was based on.

Or was I just desensitized to the teachings, and over time, it's the same as witnessing violence every day and the gunshots just stopped being scary?

But knowing that Papa was a founding member, was there even an experiment at all or was that part of his lie? Do the notes and findings he spoke about writing even exist? And if they do exist, where would I find them? He had an office here at The Reich, next to Darius's in a large outer building behind the warehouse. Maybe, if I could break in and find them, I could answer a lot of questions behind his reasoning for any of this because being a founder of a racist hate group doesn't make logical sense and my dad was nothing if not logical.

Or did I never really know him at all?

I'm standing in the cafeteria/gym area that serves as the Reich's meeting room. Percy is beside me while Darius stands behind a pulpit on the small stage, preaching to his followers. A twisted deacon spewing lies that his followers are eating up like eager mice feasting on dumpster scraps.

I tune out his voice and focus on my feet. Usually, I listen and observe and make mental notes to write in my notebook, the one I hide below the false bottom of my dresser drawer, at a later time, but today, my heart can't take it.

It isn't until the meeting is over that I finally tune in. The crowd chants loudly after Darius with their hands in the air, the Nazi salute. The slogans aren't even original. They're derived from the Ku Klux Klan. Even their brand of racism isn't original.

. . .

Make America white again! The purity, the power! From blood and bone! Love it or leave it! America first! White pride!

I'm disgusted with myself when it's all over, feeling dirty for even being in the same room as the words that fill it. I feel something else, too, something I've never felt before because I've always thought of myself as one of the good guys, in this for the science of it all, but the feeling tugs at my heart, and when I stand to leave the room, I stop and take a deep breath. Guilt. What I'm feeling is pure guilt.

"Michaela," Darius calls over to me.

"Yeah?" I ask, turning around.

"Your next assignment is recruitment. Bring someone to the barbecue tomorrow."

I swallow hard. "No problem," I answer confidently while I'm screaming on the inside. It's bad enough that I've sat idly by and allowed this hatred to continue for the sake of knowledge, but now I'm being forced to drag another poor soul into this hell?

Remember your sister.

"Good. Make sure that you do," Darius says, sounding very much like a warning. He leaves the safety of his pulpit and heads out the back door toward his office.

When the crowd clears, I wait until the last person is gone and then step out into the empty hallway to do a mental self-check. It's something that victims of brainwashing are taught to do after they experience something that might trigger feelings that aren't their own or bring back memories of their experience under the thumb of those manipulating them. It's part of the deprogramming process, but I've always used it in order to avoid the actual programming.

How am I feeling?

Well, I feel like the rug has been pulled out from under me. I feel like a failure. I feel like Darius's popularity and that of the Reich is flourishing while I'm falling, mid-flail with my arms spinning in the air in a pointless attempt to keep myself from crashing ass-first to the ground.

I feel like for someone who knows so much, it turns out that I know nothing at all.

Like what I've been focusing on, the science of it all, doesn't matter anymore. But what does?

Love matters.

My sister matters.

Pike matters.

I look around the now empty room and take in the walls that house all the lies that make up what the Fourth Reich stands for.

It's funny, you know, if you can find humor in racism and what not, that from a psychology standpoint, most people join groups like this not to join a community of shared values. They adapt the values of the group in which they perceive they will find acceptance. While the group itself, by its very definition, is anti-acceptance.

Back at the university, there is a word we had for these people.

Idiots.

I find myself in a long, narrow hallway covered with framed photos, plaques, and other Fourth Reich memorabilia. It's their entire history laid out in an elaborate collage.

Someone has Pinterest.

The history of hatred.

That's what I'm going to call this hallway. The place where The Fourth Reich has proudly mounted their perceived accomplishments and felonies for their fellow members to see. Their version of trophies displayed in a glass case. Blue ribbons for the most closed-minded.

A lot of the frames contain clippings from newspapers. Articles about the Reich showing up at peaceful rallies to instigate riots. To enrage the already enraged. The included pictures are mostly of white, caped men yelling in the faces of equally determined darker skinned faces, guilty only of wanting their voices to be heard and hoping the Reich would sit back and allow them to speak.

There are other articles, too. Sickening acts of violence against people of color framed here as proud admission of responsibility.

My stomach churns, but I force myself to keep reading. To know their motivations so I can use it against them.

Each article, picture, flag, or quote is more sickening than the last.

At one end of the long hall hang black and white photos that as you get further down morph into faded color then brighten towards the end.

The white capes. The groups of men women and children all giving the Nazi salute to the camera.

The phrase FOURTEEN WORDS is painted in script at the top of the wall. The first slogan of many lining the hallway. I know what it means. I've heard it a lot over the years, but I've always looked at it and at their propaganda with a scientific mind. Words spoken by, essentially, mentally ill people. I've tried to analyze why they feel this way and what their chemical makeup looks like under a microscope and the crowds' responses to certain trigger words, but I've never stopped and really thought about the words themselves. What they mean. "We must secure the existence of our people and a future for white children." That's what 'fourteen words' means. Fourteen sickening fucking words. SWP follows it. Supreme white power.

I hold my stomach as I move on, and as I do, the images only grow more terrifying. I knew all of this was wrong, but did I really feel it? Did I ever feel the empathy for the targets of their hatred like I should have? If I did, I don't remember.

Fuck. I'm just like my father. Cold and unfeeling.

Which makes sense now because you have to be cold and unfeeling to regard the majority of the world's population as inferior to yourself. As nothing more than rats in the street.

The end of the hall is decorated in flags. The confederate flags I was once told were a symbol of southern pride, I now realize are symbols of the losing side of the civil war. It's akin to hanging a swastika, which, I look up, is hanging directly above it.

My knees are weak as I reach the end of the hall. All of the things I used to think were just symbols of ignorance are not just a result of a lack of knowledge or information. Just the opposite. They had all of the knowledge. All of the information. All of the history. The Reich simply chooses to see things as they want to see them. They choose to hate.

I stagger back from the hall, the trophies hanging there, showing their history of hate blurs then becomes clear. Clearer than they've ever been.

These things used to not be a factor for me. These terrible things that used to be okay with me for the sake of science aren't fucking okay anymore.

They should burn along with the rest of this fucking place, and not just because I'm seeking revenge. Revenge is still coming but pales in comparison to the now bigger and much more painful picture laid out for me in fucking collage-style.

I cannot fight The Reich just for my own selfish purposes anymore. My family's murders are just the tip of the iceberg when it comes to how many lives they've ruined. How many innocent people they've terrorized. How many children they've turned into monsters,

Children like Percy.

My war has a bigger meaning. A bigger purpose.

And that purpose isn't just revenge. It's humanity.

The world is a blur around me as I rush through the compound and into my room. I close the door and lean my back against it. With my eyes shut, I release a long exhale. "You'll find her. She'll be okay," I whisper to myself. "You can do this. You just need a plan."

"Talking to yourself is a common symptom of schizophrenia," a voice suddenly muses. "At least, that's what I learned in prison."

My eyes snap open to find Percy, sitting on my bed with his back to me. His white tank top stretched over his back, his head bowed.

"It can also be a sign of high-functioning cognitive behavior," I reply on instinct. "Why are you in my room?" I shift from one foot to the other, then correct myself, straightening my shoulders and taking the stance of someone who isn't guilty of anything.

Percy spins around to face me, and my eyes immediately drop to what he's holding on his lap. A book. No, a journal. My body grows cold. *No. It can't be…*

But it is.

Percy is holding my journal.

.

7

MICKEY

EVERY WORD I've ever written about the Reich is in Percy's hands. Every analysis I've made about its members, about Darius.

About him.

"Where did you get that?" I ask, looking to the dresser. The drawer I keep it in is open, the false bottom hanging haphazardly over the side.

He ignores my question because the answer is obvious. He found it right where I put it. "This has all been some sort of experiment to you?" Percy slams the journal shut.

I jump, startled. "It's…it's not what you think," I stammer, trying to figure out what to say and find the words to use that are somehow going to get me out of this alive. I study his body language. His tight jaw and dark beady eyes tell me that he's either excited or fucking pissed, and considering what he's just read, I'm going with the latter.

"All this time," he says, standing from the bed. The ferocity of his hard gaze causes my spine to grow rigid. He shakes his head and smirks. "Right under my fucking nose."

He rubs his palms over the stubble on his head. "It's all been a fucking lie. You. This was all for research? To discover what makes us tick? It's been a fucking game to you!" A thick, blue vein pulses in his throat, giving a heartbeat to the swastika tattoo covering his Adam's Apple.

"You're judging *me*?" I laugh, even though it's not the *haha* kind of funny. But there's no denying it now. I can't hide from my words, my confession written in my own clear legible handwriting.

His chest heaves. He balls his fists. "Answer me! Has this all been a fucking game to you?"

"No," I say. "Games are fun. None of this has been fun."

"I thought…" He looks to the ceiling, then back to me. "I thought you were my friend. We've known each other since we were kids. You betrayed me." There's a hurt in his words that I never expected to hear. Not from Percy, not ever.

"How did you ever think that we were friends? We were pushed together by our fathers. We never had a conversation that wasn't about the Reich." I wave my hands in the air wildly, feeling every bit as frustrated as I do afraid. "You don't even know me."

"But, you know me, right?" He stalks toward the window and rests his hands on the sill. "A true sociopath, exhibiting all of the traits in which a sociopath is classically defined. Those behaviors have flourished under the lamp lights provided by the perfect breeding ground, courtesy of the environmental and social factors found within The Fourth Reich," he recites, throwing my words back at me. "So, Michaela, you ask a lot of questions in that book of yours. You've made a lot of obser-vations, but tell me, what is it that you've actually learned? Tell me what you've discovered during your time here observing us. Observing me. Did you find out *the reasons we hate?"* Disgust rolls off of his lips when he emphasizes the title of my research.

He turns from the window and stalks toward me, stopping in the middle of the room, pinning me in place with his dark glare.

I swallow hard, but I don't back down. If I'm going to die it's going to be with the truth on my lips.

"No more lies," Percy grates. "Tell me what you've learned."

I straighten my shoulders. "I've learned that hate is a disease like any other human affliction, but deadlier. I've learned that kindness is the only cure, but it's rejected by your kind and not even considered an option."

"And why is that?" he asks, crossing his arms over his chest.

I hold his gaze and return it with a fiery one of my own. "You reject the concept of kindness and love because hate is an easier option. It's more constant. Love is hard. It fluctuates. It's erratic and unreliable. It takes work you are all too fucking lazy to put in because you're too busy living your life as fucking monsters."

"That doesn't sound very educational. Are those the exact words you're going to use in your paper?"

I don't answer because there will never be a finished paper. Not anymore.

"And you think Pike is better than me?"

My eyes widen.

"Yeah, I know about the two of you, but I've already told you I suspected as much. Don't deny it. I know Pike. You'd be dead otherwise." He flexes his knuckles. "You don't think that he's taken a life out of anger? Because if you think the answer is no, you'd be wrong. He has. What makes one monster different from another?" He tilts his head like he's not just asking this as a rhetorical question, but as if he actually wants to know the answer.

So, I tell him.

"Love isn't perfect, and neither is Pike. But, at least, his anger is productive. It fuels the actions that he carries out in defense of his business, and to protect those he's loyal to. It's not misplaced, like yours, or a product of believing in a truth that isn't based in logic or fact. His violence may not be right either, but it's validated. It's a reaction. And unlike you, he doesn't provoke. His goals aren't to cause chaos or hurt innocent people. He doesn't act out of ignorance or blatant racism. You want to know what the difference is between monsters? One lurks in the dark and only comes out when necessary; the other puts on a costume and parades about like they're in some kind of pageant, putting on a show for the world to see. To fear. But then again, it probably makes it a lot easier to hate people if you make them hate you first."

Percy searches my eyes, for what I'm not exactly sure. Maybe, he's just seeing me for the first time for who and what I really am. In his eyes, a traitor. I hold my breath, waiting for a blow, a decision, a death sentence to be dealt.

I'm surprised when he steps away instead. "So, little Michaela Lovejoy finally decided to grow some balls," he muses.

"What are you going to do to me?" I ask, my chest heaving my muscles clenched in fear.

"Oh Mickey," he chuckles, before suddenly stepping back. He tosses my notebook on the bed and smiles, opening his arms wide. "I'm going to join you."

"Join me?" I ask, rubbing my wrists. "Join me in what?" I

ask, swallowing hard. This is the end. I've been found out. There will be no going back from this moment.

"You know what." Percy spins around the room, arms stretched out, pointing to the walls and then the ceiling. He smirks. "In bringing it all down."

In every prank show, there's a moment where the person being pranked stands there silent and stunned, unsure of what exactly is going on, how to proceed, what's real and what's not.

That's the moment I'm living in. I have no idea how I got to it or what really just happened. Did Percy just ask to join me in taking down the Fourth Reich?

The seconds pass, moving in slow motion. If this is a prank, it's a pretty shitty one, at least for me. Percy and Darius are the most manipulative men alive. I'm not about to confess everything and get myself killed before I've had a chance to carry out my plans. No, I'm keeping my cards close to my chest, out of view, in case this is some sort of trick or a test. That's it. I'll think of it as a test.

I'm good at those. Tests are my jam.

A's all the way, baby.

"Uh, Percy?" I start, giving him my best *I don't know what you're talking about* face. "Bringing what down? What do you think I've got planned?" I'm playing dumb. Well, at the very least, ignorant. I may have just admitted to being with Pike but I'm not about to admit that I have a plan to take down the organization he was born into.

"Playing dumb ain't gonna work on me, Mickey. I know how smart you are, and I know what you're planning," he insists.

Fuck.

"Did someone put something in your head, and tell you —"

Percy cuts me off. "No one told me shit. I know what you're up to because I recognize myself in your eyes. I couldn't see it before, not until I changed and started seeing everything differently. We want the same things, Mickey. To end it. *All* of it." He sits down on the edge of the bed. The usual hate-filled eyes I'm used to seeing glaring at me are gone, replaced with a much more tired version. And he's right. I see myself in his eyes.

"When?" I ask, pushing off the wall and joining him on the bed. "When did you change?"

He sighs and looks down at his hands. . "When I was in prison. I...I just changed my mind. I saw clearly for the first time. Things, people, the world, but mostly myself. It all became...clear. For the first time."

"Why?" I press, curious as to what can change beliefs he's lived his entire life upholding and wondering if whatever changed him can be sucked into a syringe and injected into the rest of them.

"Why?" he laughs. "Because I feel like shit all the time. Because I was, *am*, angry all the time. I'm tired of being angry. Of being this person."

"How do I know you're telling me the truth and this isn't some sort of elaborate trap to get me to confess?" I ask, cautiously.

Percy pulls a bandana from his back pocket and swipes at the back of his neck. When he pulls it away, it's covered with ink and the tattoo is smeared across his skin, revealing scarred raised ink-free skin underneath. "There's this program in the joint," he starts, "to help inmates rid themselves of the tattoos from gangs and hate groups. To erase the symbols that link us to our past. I started with my head and the ones on my neck are mostly gone now. I'll eventually do the rest of my body, but it takes a long time and a lot of sessions to get them to go away and as much as I don't want to sound like a fucking pussy, it hurts like a son of a bitch."

"That's why you're growing your hair back," I realize, pointing to the blonde stubble on his head.

Percy rubs his palm over it. "Yeah, also, you know that the men of The Reich are supposed to grow their hair out when they get married. Skinheads are the soldiers, and Darius has always wanted me to be a leader. Our marriage is supposed to solidify that, and I guess it doesn't hurt that I won't have to have April painting my head every morning."

"That's the girl who is always coming out of your room in the morning? I thought…"

He raises an eyebrow. "You thought she was one of the Reich's girls? A whore?"

"I was going to say consenting sexual participant working to meet the needs of the men of The Reich," I correct.

"Of course, you were," he laughs. "Well, good. I guess if someone has to see her coming out, it's not bad that's the impression they got, but no, she's a makeup artist. She does the one on the back of my neck and the one on my throat. The ones I wouldn't be able to hide, even with a full head of hair." He looks down at his colorful arms, sleeves of bigotry displayed in beautiful colorful art. "I still have a lot of work to do," he sighs. "And I'm glad these are gone." He runs his fingers over his throat, head and neck, but I can still feel them there. I can remove them from my skin but the reason I want to take down the Reich is because I want them gone from here," he places his open hand against his chest. "It's going to take more than a few sessions with a laser to remove those."

"What do you want from all this? What's the reason you came back here after prison?" I ask.

His eyes are both determined and sad.

"Redemption."

There's a knock at the door. "Michaela," a voice calls out. "Darius wants to see you to talk about the recruitment."

"You better go," Percy says. "We'll talk more later."

I turn to leave, then stop. "How...how is she?" I ask, because I have to.

"She's safe...for now."

8

PIKE

THE DOOR to King's studio is unlocked. It squeaks and groans as I push past it and enter the dimly lit, unoccupied room.

Again, I check the message King sent me. It ordered me to be here at eight PM.

I'm a few minutes early, so while I wait, I take in the room around me. Two giant windows line the back wall, lighting the room in what's left of the setting sun's rays. Below the windows are a row of black shiny toolboxes with a butcher block counter resting over the top. A backlit easel sits upon the counter with a stack of fresh stencils in the small open drawer beneath.

I follow the direction of the new-looking multi-tone grey wood floors into the center of the room where a big, comfortable black leather couch and chairs divide the workspaces on each side with a low glass coffee table between.

Each workspace consists of a tattoo table, swivel stool, and an additional tool box like on the back wall, except these are on wheels.

The wall over one of the workspaces catches my eye. It's

covered in a graffiti version of the landscape of Logan's Beach, complete with a tiny, spray-painted cock and balls on the water tower. I chuckle to myself that Preppy's vandalism made it into such a work of art. Looking over the rest of the town, I can even make out the rooftop of my pawn shop. The details are incredible, but then again, I couldn't draw the cock and balls on the water tower, never mind a masterpiece mural like this one. So, I may not be the best person to judge art for the exception of maybe how much it's worth. I spin on my heel and continue on to the other side of the room where the art covering almost every inch of space in an intricate collage is different than the mural and yet somehow even more incredible. They're mostly canvas black and white portraits, close-ups of women's faces or faceless nudes. I recognize one of the faces as Poe, Nine's girl, and another as Thia, Bear's wife.

My chest constricts when I see Mickey's face staring back at me from one of the portraits. Suddenly, I can't breathe. I plop down onto one of the chairs and rest my elbows on my knees, rubbing my palms over my face. Mickey isn't up on that wall, I remind myself. When I look up again, the portrait is no longer Mickey, but Dre, Preppy's wife.

And I thought Mickey was crazy for seeing things.

As the sun sets further into the horizon, the studio begins to glow. The LED rope lighting lining the room casts the walls and floors in shades of neon green and orange. The soffit above the windows has a sign that reads *King's Tattoo*, on a neon sign depicting a skull wearing a crown and a bow tie with the number nine in the center. The skull is symbolic of Bear, the crown of King, the bow tie of Preppy, and the Nine in the middle is a recent addition, for of course, Nine himself.

I find myself staring back at the mural again and

wondering if I'll ever be able to prove myself in this town. I don't even hear King until he's standing directly behind me. "I'm the one who painted it, and even I find myself staring at this shit all too often," he says.

I turn my head to see him with his big arms crossed over his chest. The neon lights cause the spikes on the belts wrapped around his arms to glow bright white.

"I don't know shit about art," I admit with a shrug, "beyond what it's worth. I couldn't tell you if something is good or bad, but just looking at this shit, I have to say it's pretty fucking amazing."

"Not nearly as good as my girl's stuff," he points to the other wall with his smoke. "She's got the real gift. I can make something look good, while Ray—" He smirks and shakes his head as if he can't believe it himself. He absentmindedly rubs his thumb over a tattoo of a black bird on the back of his hand. "Her shit makes you feel something. That's real fucking talent." His voice is filled with pride and wonder. Again, I find myself thinking about Mickey. If things were different, would I be speaking about her the same way? Doesn't matter. She made her choice, and I'll never find out. I try to shake off the thought, but it's like shaking off a tick that's already half-burrowed into your skin. Hard to get rid of and might cause an incurable disease. In my case? The disease is love.

Love?

I...shit. I *do* love her. I'm fucking in love with her.

I remember my earlier revelation with Thorne. It doesn't matter that Mickey made her choice, because I plan on making another one for her.

"You got something you want to get off of your mind?" King asks, cocking an eyebrow that's missing half the pigment on one side.

I run my hand through my hair and blow out a breath. "I wouldn't know where to start. Talking's never been my thing. I thought we'd go over a plan I have for the Reich. There's been a development."

King pulls out a bottle of Jack Daniel's from the bottom cabinet of one of the tool boxes and nods to the skull shot glasses on the coffee table. I retrieve two of them, and he fills both. We clink our glasses together before downing our shots. The liquid burns on the way down but not enough to burn out the longing that grows inside of me with each passing hour.

"Talkin' ain't never been my gig, either. I speak when I've got something to say, and usually, it's only when I'm pissed. But with the kids and Ray, it's different. It turns out if someone calls "Daddy" forty-five times in a row, they'll still keep goin' until you respond." He smirks and pours two more shots. "What's this plan of yours?"

I lay it out for him, and he nods. "It's a solid plan. Complicated as fuck, but so is the situation." His eyes meet mine, and one side of his mouth curls up in a knowing half-smile. "So, you've decided to claim her, after all. You realize you're responsible for her now. As much as it means that we can't lay a hand on her in any way, it also means that any actions of Mickey's that affects us comes back on you. And you can't take that shit back. You only get one claim."

I nod because I know there's no going back. I don't want to go back. "I understand how it works. Mickey's mine."

King downs the next shot, and I follow his lead. "You know," he starts, staring into his empty shot glass. "I get pissed off a lot when shit goes sideways, but that's only because I have high expectations of the people I choose to surround myself with. You, included."

I sigh. "Yeah, and I've been doing a lot of fucking up lately. I know."

He sets down the glass. "You don't think I've fucked up before?" He smirks. "There was a time when alls I did was fuck up. Especially, when I first started out. Hell, I went to the clink so many times I was starting to think they'd give me one of them frequent customer cards or some shit. I fucked up more shit than I got right." He looks at a picture of his family on top of the tool box. "Even managed to get myself locked up for a few years. Got myself separated from the only thing that mattered at the time. My baby girl, Max."

Max is the one that Darius tried to take from King through her birth mother all in the name of causing a rift between me and King. "I can't imagine what it was like when she…when the shit hit the fan during the hurricane."

"No, you can't, but you will, someday. His voice changes from sad to determined. He points at my chest. "You gotta put that past you, and you gotta know that I give you shit because I see a lot of myself in you. The drive. The take no bullshit attitude. The fucking stare you give everyone when you know they're full of shit." He chuckles. "You wouldn't be around if I didn't want you around. I trust Nine, and I trust you. Try not to fuck it up again, but if you do, we'll work it out. That's what families do. Real fucking families. And it ain't got shit to do with blood. Though, some of that gets spilled along the way. Especially around here."

I appreciate his loyalty, but I also need him to know mine. "I'll pay you back all of the money I owe you. I'm going to sell the shop."

King frowns, and he lifts his glass again, gripping it so tight I'm surprised he doesn't break it in his hand. "No, you fucking won't. I got more money than I can bury. I lent that cash to you as an investment, and sometimes, investments don't work out. You'll pay me back, but you don't gotta do it now. And you ain't selling your fucking shop. That's final."

"I don't see any other way," I reply.

"You're a smart kid, Pike. Don't consider it an investment in the deal that went bust. Consider the cash an investment in *you*. Long term."

"But," I begin to argue.

"You love your shop, right?" King asks. He looks around his own studio. "Probably as much as I love this fucking place."

I nod. "It's the first real thing I ever owned that was truly mine."

"Then, you ain't giving it up. That's an order. You've got a future ahead of you. I'll be here when you figure your shit out, and I know you will because as I've said, I see a lot of myself in you, and I know that right now you're trying to think of a million alternative ways to pay me back, and you won't stop until you do. It wasn't your fault, but I know you'll make right by it. Try and sell it and I'll buy it back in your name and then you'll owe me even more."

He's right.

King smirks because he fucking knows he's right. "And on that note, you want a tat or something?" he asks, pouring another shot for each of us.

I down mine quickly. This time, there is no burn from the alcohol, just from the bittersweet truth trickling down my throat.

I shake my head. "Not tonight," I say, wanting to get to the point of why King wanted me to be here now that I've laid out my plans for him.

King walks over to the nearest swivel stool and takes a

seat. Even in the small chair, it's as if he's just sat upon his throne in the Kingdom that he built. "Then, did you come here just to stare at my walls, or was it just to tell me your plans and claim your girl?" he asks, lighting a cigarette and holding out the pack to me. I take one and light it as well, perplexed by his question.

"Uh, you asked me to come here," I remind him.

King shakes his head. "I got a lot going on right now, but remembering who I set a meeting with isn't something I ever forget."

I frown and reach into my back pocket, and pull out the note he sent me this morning. I hand it to King.

He takes a deep drag off his smoke. He looks from the note to me. "This wasn't me."

"Then, who?" I ask.

The door slowly creaks open.

Our eyes meet as we both realize we've been set up. King springs out of his chair and heads to the wall safe behind one of the drawings, and I draw my gun from my waistband as he pulls out a weapon of his own.

"Who the fuck is there?" King shouts, grabbing a gun from the safe he takes a position on one side of the door while I take another.

A man walks in with his hands on his head as if he's being arrested. I can only see the back of him from my position. His head is shaved down to the skin. He's wearing a white tank top and baggy jeans. He's got tattoos, shitty ones depicting swastikas and…

"Oh, shit," I whisper to myself before realizing there isn't time for hesitation when it comes to Percy Alban.

I rush forward and kick out his legs from behind, sending him to his knees. I press the gun to the back of his head.

"You've got two minutes to speak before I blow your fucking brains through your forehead."

"I'm not armed. I didn't come here to cause shit," he says, calmly. Too calmly. "I came here to talk."

"Oh yeah? Who else did you bring to have this talk?" King asks, stepping in front of Percy.

Percy shakes his head. "No one, man. Check your fucking cameras. I came in here alone."

King steps over to the monitors beside the door and checks the cameras. He nods to me. "He's tellin' the truth. He's alone."

"I told you," Percy says. "I just came here to talk."

"Why should I fucking talk to you, of all fucking people?" I grate, as King steps to the other side.

He looks over his shoulder at me. "Because I need help, from both of you." He looks to King and then to me with what looks like tears in his eyes. "And so does Mickey."

"Give me one fucking reason why I shouldn't put a bullet in your fucking head right the fuck now." I grate. "You killed Gutter, you son of a bitch."

Remembering how Gutter was murdered right before my eyes in the parking lot of my business and home. The only person and only place sacred to me ruined in one stroke of a fucking baseball bat. I gnash my teeth so hard they feel as if they're about to break. My jaw tightens. My hands shake for the first time since I was a fucking kid. The anger of the memory mixes with the sweetness of revenge, which is only one trigger pull away from being mine.

Percy shakes his head. "I didn't —"

I don't let him finish because facts are fucking facts.

94

"Don't fucking deny it!" I push the barrel of my gun against his temple. "I fucking saw you fucks with your skeleton hoodies. There ain't nothing you can say that is going to buy you a ticket out of your death sentence."

"I'm not looking for a ticket out. I wasn't there, but it was us. I should have stopped it but I didn't. But, that's not why I came here," he says, calmly. Too fucking calmly considering the adrenaline shooting through my veins is enough to bring someone long in the grave back to fucking life.

"Then, what the fuck are you looking for?" I press, seeing nothing but how good King's studio would look decorated with his fucking brains.

Percy sighs and looks to the ground. "Redemption, but I know I ain't gonna find that here." His eyes meet mine, and there's none of the rage or cockiness I'm used to seeing when our paths have crossed in the past. "I killed him. Not by my own hand but in a roundabout way. I knew it was gonna happen, and I let it. Gutter's death is on me. His blood is on my hands," he admits. "And I know it don't mean shit, but I'm sorry for it."

"You're right. It don't mean shit." I reply, smacking him in the back of his head with the handle of my gun.

"Ahhhh!" He rubs his head and hisses. "It happened because Darius told me and the rest of the Reich that Gutter was the one responsible for the death of my moms. It's not an excuse. It's just the reason. I fucking swear it."

"Next thing I know, you're going to tell me that you and your fucking clan had nothing to do with threatening King and his family all because you think I snitched on you and got you locked up," I scoff. I roll my eyes because I ain't buying it.

"No, I know that wasn't you. Well, I know that now. That shit with King and trying to get to you by threatening him and stealing your shit to put you at war with King? That was Darius. I knew that before I got out of the joint. I can't deny that because it's the fucking truth." He takes a deep breath. "But, that's not why I'm here. Like I said, it's Mickey. She needs your help."

There's a noise outside. Light footsteps on the gravel.

Motherfucking liar.

"Shit," Percy swears, his chin dropping to his chest.

"Thought you said you came alone," King remarks, cocking his gun still aimed at the back of Percy's head. "Guess you wanted a witness to your execution." King jerks his head to me, and I go to the door, listening for movement on the other side. There's a slight sound of shuffling, and all I see is the color of the blood I'm about to spill from whoever the fuck it is that Percy brought along to carry out whatever stupid fucking plan he had in mind.

Percy looks nervously to the door. "I said I came in *here* alone," he blurts out quickly. "There's someone else with me, but it's not what you—"

Fueled by anger, I turn the handle, grip my gun with both hands and kick open the door. A lump of dirty, dark hair falls at my feet.

"—think," he finishes.

She's shaking in fear, staring up at me with wide eyes.

"What the fuck did you do to her?" I accuse Percy, looking down at the shivering girl who doesn't so much as make a sound.

"Nothing, there's a monster fucking coyote lurking outside. She probably just got scared and wanted to come in. I told Mickey I'd protect her, and this is the only place I could think of that she'd be safe. Here. With you." He picks her up and sets her gingerly on the couch. "She's quiet, that's for sure. Think there's something wrong with her vocal chords. Her name is Mindy."

"As in Mickey's dead sister?" I ask, surprised.

"Yeah," he croaks. "The very one."

Said coyote's ears must have been ringing because Pancakes, who belongs to Bear, decides to make his entrance.

"See! I told you!" Percy says, pointing at Pancakes who strolls into King's studio and sniffs the air and then sniffs at Mindy. He decides that whatever is taking place isn't worth his time or effort, so he turns around and stalks off into the night.

"He's domesticated," King tells Percy.

There's a shriek in the distance, the echo of a small animal that sounds like it's being mauled to death. The sound becomes a muffled yelp before there's no noise at all.

King walks over and kicks the door shut before resuming guard over Percy. "For the most part," he adds. King picks up Mindy carefully and places her gently on the couch. She turns toward the back cushions, pressing herself against them while trembling in fear.

"Fuck, she's fucked up," King points out.

"Can we talk now?" Percy asks. "You can still kill me after. Just hear me out first."

As much as I'd like to shut him up by way of bullet in his fucking mouth, the need to hear what the fuck is going on wins out. I nod to King who pulls Percy off the floor by his shoulder and shoves him into a chair, standing guard over him.

My gun might be pointed to the floor, but my finger massages the fucking trigger while I look from Mindy to Percy.

"So, fucking talk."

9

MICKEY

Percy's been gone all night. His trailer is empty. My continued search for my sister has gotten me a whole lot of nowhere. And today, I have to find a recruit for the Reich and bring whoever the unfortunate soul winds up being, back to the compound for the barbecue later on this afternoon.

But first, there's one more place I haven't checked for Mindy. A place that's off limits to everyone in The Reich, including Percy.

Darius's office.

Mud cakes the small path that leads from the portable classroom trailers through a thick patch of woods to a small outbuilding that used to be some sort of hunter's cabin that Darius has claimed as his office and where he reigns over The Reich.

The muddy path isn't the route I take. I don't want to be seen heading toward his office plus, I don't want to raise suspicions with a trail of muddy footprints leading up to his door. Instead, I enter the wooded area by way of the open field, weaving my way through long wet grass. Ankle deep water sloshes all around me. I slow my movements so as to not cause any noticeable wake or sound. I move painfully slow, but it works. The only sound is the buzzing of mosquitoes and the occasional croaking frog.

The cabin itself isn't more than a one room log shack with a rickety front porch surrounded by an overgrowth of brush. I make my way around to the back of the building and peer into the windows. Because it's only one room it's easy to see that it's empty of all occupants. Mindy is nowhere to be found. My heart sinks, but there's a possibility that there is something in there that will lead me to her so I press on. The steps creak and groan as I make my way up to the backdoor.

Of course, it's locked, but I came prepared. Twenty minutes watching a YouTube video has given me the skills I need to pick a lock. I take out my tools, two long metal pieces I made out of a coat hanger. One straight and one with a hook at the end. It takes a few minutes longer than I expect. I'm sweating by the time the lock gives and the door sways open with a long groan.

Darius's desk takes up the majority of the room. Surprisingly there are no Fourth Reich symbols or metals like those that hang in the main building. The walls are blank for the exception of an old photograph of Darius and my father. The one Nine had showed me on the computer when we discovered that my dad and Darius had started The Reich together.

What kind of sick bastard keeps a picture in his private office of the man he is responsible for killing?

Darius. That's fucking who.

I pad over to the desk and duck behind it. The drawers are unlocked and most filled with office supplies, calendars and other clutter. Nothing useful. I move over to the file cabinet. Inside the bottom drawer is a file on every member of The

Reich along with an account of dues paid and a description of their duties.

The top drawer, however, is locked. I take out my coat hanger lock picks and this time it takes me less than a minute to crack the lock and open the drawer. Inside, I find a stack of notebooks. I lift the first one and open to the first page. Immediately, I recognize the handwriting as my father's.

May, 21ˢᵗ, 1999

The summer has just started, and Darius and I already had our first fight over some of the recruits he's obtained during the year. They're more violent than any of the previous ones. Percy is also beginning to change, and it hurts me to see this affecting him as it has. I have begged for Darius to tell him the truth, to keep him out of the experiment, but Darius insists that if I'm to study the effects of hatred and loyalty in the brain, Percy needs to be a part of it.

I don't believe this to be true. I think Darius has grown used to having Percy, not as a son, but as his personal mound of clay to mold into the lapdog he wants him to be. He's greedy, and his association with the cartel has only made him more so. It was only supposed to be to fund the experiment, but it turns out that Darius enjoys the wealth that it brings. I worry that he's grown addicted to the thrill of it all. The violence. The power.

I threatened to tell Percy myself, but Darius would not hear of it anymore. In turn, he threatened to expose me as a fraud, but that doesn't make sense to me since he would essentially be exposing himself. I remind myself that this is a long game, and it's far from over. I find myself asking how one can truly study hate without being a proponent of it?

I can't fucking breathe.

Holy shit.

Darius knew it was an experiment? They started The Reich together but not as racists looking for followers, but as an experiment. So Darius didn't kill my father because he found out he was studying The Reich.

But then, *why*?

☙

WITH MY FATHER'S JOURNAL TUCKED UNDER THE DRIVER'S seat, and his words swimming in my brain, I set out to fulfill the task Darius has placed upon me.

Today, I have to find a new recruit and bring them back to The Reich for the barbeque this afternoon.

The taste of dread dries out my mouth.

"You can do this. You can do this," I chant to myself.

Yeah, you can do this, but you don't fucking want too.

I take one of the vans belonging to The Reich and drive to a spot by the bridge close to where my family crashed into the river four years earlier. I park and try not to recall all the vivid images threatening to take over my thoughts and focus on the task at hand. I can do this. I can totally recruit someone, and then, when it's all over, I'll tell them the truth and get them the fuck out.

No harm. No foul?

Sure, just play a game with someone's life and mind. It's fine. It doesn't make you a terrible person at all.

But it does. And as much as I like to think I've been a bystander in all of this, I haven't. I helped rob Pike's shipment that night. I helped break into his shop to steal his stash.

I'm the one who shot Badger in the leg.

Twice.

The guilt I feel, though warranted, is completely unhelpful.

I take a deep breath and try to focus.

My eyes land on a girl, sitting alone on a rock, smoking a cigarette. Her bright red hair is pulled into a ponytail at the nape of her neck. Her black t-shirt and baggy jeans are several sizes too big, and her once white sneakers are dirt caked, the laces black.

I spy a camping backpack by her feet pushed up against the rock.

I approach her carefully so as not to scare her off.

"Do you live around here?" I ask.

She whips her head around to face me. Her bright green eyes dull with whatever hardship has her living out of a backpack and hanging out under the bridge. She shrugs. "I live around here...and there."

I tuck my hands in my back pockets. "Listen, I'm just about to go and grab some food. You wanna join me?"

"You part of some church group or something?" she asks, scrunching her nose.

"Nope. I'm not exactly the religious type."

She nods and takes a drag of her cigarette. "Then, do I look like I got money for food?" She shakes her head and stubs out her cigarette on the rock, flicking it into the water.

"No, it's on me. Actually, it's on my family. They're having a barbecue. You should come," I say, and the kindness in my voice isn't fake. The girl's cheeks are sunken in, and it looks like she could use a good meal. It's the least I can do for her, considering where I'm taking her and what I'm potentially exposing her to.

It's all part of the greater plan.

"Why?" she asks, suspiciously, and rightfully so.

I take a few steps toward her. "Well, because you look lost and I was lost once, and before you can find yourself, you have to feed yourself," I explain. "Besides, someone gave me a second chance once. Someone gave me hope when I didn't have any."

And it's true, but I'm not thinking of the Reich when I say those words. I'm talking about Pike.

She raises a suspicious, pierced eyebrow.

I smile. "Maybe, I just want to return the favor to the universe, pay it forward. Some shit like that."

She shakes her head. "Nah, I'm good. I don't feel like being sex- trafficked today."

"You got a phone?" I ask.

She nods slowly. "Yeah, why?"

"Take it out." I take a step back. "I'm not trying to take it from you I swear."

Reluctantly, she pulls it out of her pocket.

I turn to the side and pose the way the girls do these days with their selfies. Hand on my hip, knee up, slightly turned to the side. "Take a picture of me."

She rolls her eyes and laughs. She takes a picture of my ridiculous pose. She laughs harder when I give full duck lips. "You going to leave now?"

"No, I want you to send that picture to someone you trust along with my name. Michaela Lovejoy. Dr. Michaela Love-joy, actually. I'll give you the address of the barbecue, too, and if the person you are texting likes barbecue, then invite them to come along."

She twists her lips and then her thumbs fly over the keys, and I know she'll be coming back with me.

I smile brighter. "Make sure to tell them if you go missing that I'm the one responsible."

I almost forget that my plans are actually nefarious when we're in the van singing along to a bubbly pop song until she lowers the volume and asks, "So, what's the name of this group of yours?"

It takes everything I have to maintain a casual attitude and to keep the smile on my face from dropping, but the corner of my lip twitches with disdain. "The Fourth Reich."

"Never heard of it," she says, staring out the window at the cornfields surrounding the road. "My name's Emma, by the way."

"Nice to meet you, Emma," I reply. The van makes a dinging sound. "Shit. I need gas," I say, noticing the red line is below empty. I pull into the Stop-N-Shop. "Wait in here. I'll just be a second."

I step out of the van and go inside, paying for the gas. When I come back out, I fill the tank. I replace the gas nozzle on the hook, and when I turn back around, I find myself trapped, barricaded by a wall of Pike.

"What?" I breathe. "What the hell are you doing here?"

"I can ask you the same thing," he says, looking toward the truck. "Who the fuck is that?"

"Nobody," I reply. I want to be mean and rude and yell at him but staring up into his eyes I feel the pull between us and I can't ignore it.

"I thought I'd never see you again," I whisper.

He stares into my eyes. "You thought wrong." He points to the van. "Who the fuck is that?"

I bounce my weight from one foot to another, not wanting to tell him. Embarrassed and ashamed.

"Mic," he presses, pushing me against the back of the van. He brushes a stray hair away from my face. "Tell me....please"

I look to my shoes. "Fine. She's my assignment. I have to bring a recruit back to the barbecue," I say, quickly. I cross my arms over my chest like a child. "Happy? Because I'm not."

He frowns. "Far fucking from it."

"It's not like I want to," I whisper-hiss. "You think I want to bring anyone there?"

Pike rounds the van to the passenger side.

"What the fuck are you doing?" I call after him.

He ignores me and yanks the door open. Emma almost falls out, bracing herself on the seat, her red hair blowing in the breeze.

"Who the fuck are you?" she asks.

"Here, kid." Pike says, passing her several hundred-dollar bills from his wallet.

She looks at the money and then to Pike, making a slow appraisal of his long, lean body. She bites her lip. "'Cause you don't gotta pay me, baby. I'll do you for free." She laughs. "Shit, if I had any money, I'd pay you."

Pike ignores her comment and looks her in the eyes. "The place the lady here is taking you to is a racist organization hellbent on terrorizing anyone who isn't the right shade of pale," he says, honestly. "They are trying to recruit you into a life that's going to lead you down a path that will probably end with you getting locked up or killed. The money is for you to get the fuck out of this van. Use it to go home, and if that ain't an option for you, I own the Pawn Shop on main. Pike's Pawn. I've got a cot and a job for you if you're interested. Just ask for Thorne. She'll set you up."

Emma slowly takes the money as if Pike is about to snatch it back. She hurries out of the van and slams the door behind her. She looks between me and Pike. "Ya'll are a weird-ass couple," she remarks.

Before I can correct her that we aren't a couple, she scurries off toward the bus station bench. "I'll be taking you up on that offer!"

Pike nods and turns back to me. He takes me by the elbow and walks me behind the Stop-N-Shop "What the fuck are you doing, Mic?"

"What the fuck are *you* doing?" he shoots back.

"I can't go back there without a recruit. It's one of my tests."

"Then, don't go back there," he says as if it's just that simple.

"I can't because..."

"Because why?" he demands.

He spins me so my back is flush against the stucco of the building. I'm breathing heavy and my face is flushed. "Because I realized recently that all of this is about more than my revenge. It's about righting the wrongs my father put in place. I can't just kill Darius and Percy. I have to take down the Reich. Dismantle them from the inside. But there's so much I don't know. So much I still have to find out before I can do anything." I fill him in on my father's journal and Percy's odd behavior after he found mine. "And plus, Mindy is somewhere in the Reich, but Percy moved her, and I can't find her."

Pike doesn't appear as shocked as I thought he'd be at the fact that I just told him my sister, who I thought to be dead, was somewhere alive and hidden somewhere in the compound. "Tell me your plan, and tell me now," Pike demands, pressing his knee between my legs. The anger from his eyes fades. "I didn't ask you last time. I need to know. Tell me how you are going to take them down once you get the information you need."

My fingers twitch to touch him but I keep my hands

pressed to the wall by my side because I know that once I do I might not be able to form a coherent thought. "One, discover the main source of The Reich's funding and cut it off. Two, find proof of my father's lies and any skeletons in Darius's closet and expose them to the members of the Reich. Three —"

"Kill Darius," Pike finishes for me.

"And possibly Percy," I add. "That would be it," I say, laying it all out on the line. In order to live by my set of truths, I need Pike to know where my heart is. To be the one person who knows who I really am.

Even if sometimes, I'm not sure myself.

"You sure there's no talking you out of this?" Pike asks. "Because me and my boys can take them out. You can just come home with me. Right now."

"I want to," I admit. "You have no idea how much I want to do just that, but this is bigger than me now." I shake my head. "My current problem is that I can't go back to the Reich without a recruit, and you just gave mine a bunch of money and told her to fuck off." I sigh and let my head fall onto his shoulder. "But I can't help being glad that you did."

Pike rests his head against mine then lifts it. His eyes wide with an idea. "I've got a solution."

"What?" I ask, hopefully.

"It's not a what. It's a who," he says. "You've met her before."

Instantly, I know who he's talking about. "No, not her. Not again."

Pike smiles and I want to both kiss him and smack him for being so smug.

"I wish you would just stay out of this so I don't have to worry about you getting caught up in my mess!" I cry. As the words leave my lips, I know it's not true. Yes, I want to keep

Pike safe, but no I don't want him to stay out of it. Not really. I need all the help I can get and Pike is the only person alive that I trust.

He rubs the pad of this thumb over my lips and they part on instinct. "It ain't just your mess, Mic. Although it's cute to think you caused all this shit. It's just as much mine as it is yours and whether you like it or not I don't give a fuck. I'm going to help you. Help us. And you're going to let me," he brushes his lips over mine.

My entire body trembles. "Why would I do that?"

"Because, deep inside you want to, and if that's not enough," he traces his lips over the sensitive skin of my ear. "Because I have Mindy."

10

MICKEY

I BURST into Percy's trailer unannounced and slam the door shut behind me, leaning against it, out of breath and dizzy.

Percy is on the bed, laying over the blankets, perched against the headboard with an open notebook in his lap and a pen pressed to the corner of his mouth. "You just get chased or something?" he asks, placing his pen between the pages and closing the book, pushing it off his lap onto the bed.

Chased out from the fucking dark, maybe.

"Why does Pike have Mindy?" I blurt.

Percy smiles. "Because he won't hurt her, and because you trust him. I didn't want her around these people, and I made you a promise. Lord knows what would happen to her here. Thought you might like to see her at Pike's when all this shit is over."

"You went there? To see Pike?" I ask breathlessly. "And he didn't kill you? Why?" I'm yelling at him because I'm angry although I'm not sure if it's because he went and brought Pike and my sister together without telling me or because he risked his life to do so. Either way, it was an impressive move and very brave, but I can't help the anger exploding from within me from all of the unanswered questions that keep mounting on top of one another with each tick of the clock.

He shrugs. "I told him that I'm on your side. I told him everything. Plus, we made a deal."

"What kind of deal?" I demand to know with a hand on my hip.

"The kind of deal that will take place when this is all over. He agreed."

"But why are you on my side? When did you become this person? You haven't told me shit," I blurt, growing frustrated at not knowing, and irritated that I've been left in the dark.

Although, relieved that my sister is at Pike's.

She's safe. She's finally safe.

"Sit. I'll tell you." Percy pats the bed beside him, and I take a seat. He pulls out a picture from between the pages of the notebook and passes it to me. It's of a beautiful woman with bright brown eyes and a smile that could knock a man to his knees. "She's gorgeous," I say out of admiration.

"I know," he says with a sigh, tucking the picture back into his journal then shoving the journal into a drawer.

"I hate to point out the obvious, but she's a cop," I say, referring to her dark blue uniform.

He chuckles. "Corrections Officer," he says, with pure pride in his voice. "I'm surprised you didn't mention that she's also black."

"I was waiting for you on that one," I say. "How did you two meet?"

He smiles. "She was one of the Corrections Officers in the prison. She was assigned to my cell block"

My eyes widen in surprise. "Well, now that's shocking. Continue."

He tucks his hands beneath his head and leans back into the memory, staring up at the ceiling. "They can be pretty mean and rough to the inmates who deserve it, and I sure fucking deserved it. She used to kick the shit out of me almost daily, but it wasn't nothing I didn't have coming to me. One day, I was bleeding and broken and bruised, and I was still giving her attitude, still looking for more punishment when she put her nightstick away and offered me a deal. I go to a meeting. One of those groups that help people get out of gangs and shit. Once a week. I didn't have to participate, and I didn't have to believe in the shit. I just had to go, and the beatings would stop, and she would let me say whatever the fuck I wanted to say to her."

"So, you took the deal?"

He turns his head toward me. "I would have been a fool not to, but she got one over on me. I went to the first meeting, sat in the back, and tuned out. Well, until she walked in and took the podium."

"What did she say?"

There's a distant look in his eyes as he recalls the memory. "She started to explain the kind of shit she faced every day. Not just for being black but also for being law enforcement. She explained how her little brother was killed when he knocked on a door asking for help with his broke down car, and how her other brother was killed because he joined a gang that fed him lies about belonging when he was expendable to them. A pawn to protect the king. How he was brainwashed. How much it hurt her and how much she hated him when all he needed was to reach out to her. How other black people from her community, including members of her own family, won't speak to her because she's a Corrections Officer and a lot of them distrust anyone in law enforcement." He sighs. "She blamed herself for her brother's death, and the reason she chose her line of work was to make a difference in the system. To promote change. We couldn't be more different but I recognized a lot in her story as my own." He smiles from ear to ear. "She's the bravest fucking person I've ever met. Strong right hook, too." He rubs his jaw at the memory.

"And that's what did it? That's what made you change?" I ask, curiously.

He sits back up. "Nobody can make you change, but she's the one who made me begin to think twice about my life. I realized I was disobeying her and practically begging for daily beatings because I liked her attention, you know, in a perverted kind of way. I didn't realize I actually liked her. Never thought we'd be able to relate...until we did. I don't just like her." He laughs at the absurdity of it all. "I fucking love her, Mickey."

"I'm...really proud of you, Percy."

"Trust me, the shock you're feeling is nowhere near the shock I was feeling." He laughs, then looks at me. "What, the doctor ain't got shit else to say? None of them fancy words of yours floating around in that big brain right now? Thought you'd at least give me some with more syllables than I have fingers. I admit, I'm kind of disappointed."

"Watch it. Maybe, one day you and..."

"Benita. It means blessed," he laments.

"Well, maybe one day we will live in a post Fourth Reich world. One where you and Benita will live in a house, and I'll live in one nearby. We will be neighbors. I'll come over on Sundays for dinner," I say, imagining what that kind of life would look like.

"It's a nice thought. You and I both know it's not likely, but it is a nice thought…but why aren't we coming over to your place for dinner?"

"It's Sunday, my day off. I don't want to cook," I joke.

Percy lights another cigarette with the burning end of the butt in his hand. "It's a deal, but why aren't you including Pike in this? Don't you mean you and Pike's house?"

I grow quiet as the sadness takes over. "No, Pike has a life. A good one. My shit is a heavy weight to carry, and I'm not the easiest person in the world. He'd be…"

"Don't you dare say he'd be better off without you because that ain't true. No one would be better off without you, Doctor Michaela Lovejoy."

"I guess only time will tell," I say, not wanting to argue.

"Now, where are them big words about me and Benita?" he goads.

I punch him playfully in the shoulder, grateful for the change in subject. "No big words today, but I can tell you honestly that as your faux fiancé, I'm very happy that you're in love with another woman."

He punches me back. "And as your…whatever you just said that I'm assuming means fake fiancé, I can tell you that I'm very happy that you're in love with another man. Even if it is Pike."

"If only all couples could live in such blissful honesty," I say, resting my head against his shoulder.

"All couples aren't as fucked up as we are," he says, wrapping an arm over my shoulder and kissing the top of my head.

"Too-fucking-che."

Percy wrinkles his nose. "Is that French for *I agree that we are fucked*?"

I nod. "It sure as hell is."

"Hey, look at that. I'm bilingual now." He laughs.

The laughter quickly fades to silence. We sit here on the bed, leaning against each other, watching the sunset through the window while wondering what the future might hold for us and our seemingly impossible dream.

If any at all.

"I really would like to meet her someday," I tell him.

"I'm not bringing her around this shit. I'm not even going to see her until I'm a hundred percent clear, and I know no one will come after me. I can't put her in that kind of danger." He shakes his head. "I won't."

"Just like I didn't want to drag Pike into it," I agree. "That didn't work."

"No," he says, sitting up and pushing me off of his shoulder. "It's not the same."

"How isn't it the same? We both don't want the people we love involved in our shit."

"Because Benita is a civilian. I mean, she's a Corrections Officer, but she's not in this life. Pike is. Always has been. You keeping him away is like telling a thunderstorm to hold the rain. He was born for this shit. He's already in this shit. He lives it. You have a loaded gun in your pocket, and you're using it as a doorstop. You don't need to protect him. You need to use him."

I raise an eyebrow. "Would you say the same thing if Benita was Pike in this situation?"

"Hell fucking no, but she's not." Pike settles me back on his shoulder. "So, I can."

"What do you want me to do, Percy?" I ask, but what I'm really asking is, "What should I do?"

"You should talk to him. Figure it out. See what he wants, and respect it just like he's respected what you want although

I'm sure it's eating him up inside not to storm in here and blow my fucking head off."

"You don't know that," I argue.

"I do. He fucking told me, besides, if you were him and he was telling you not to get involved, wouldn't it eat you up?"

I cringe. "I hate it when you're right. Stop it. It's very unbecoming."

"Get used to it. I'm going to try to be more right from here on out."

I grab his earlobe and give it a tug. "Alright, alright. Quit it. Nobody told me that being friends with your fake fiancé would be so annoying. I think I'll trade you in for a goat."

"I'm worth at least three goats. And we already have a dog."

Bruno is the Reich's guard dog who patrols the grounds at night. I make a note to be nicer to him and maybe slip him some leftovers since I've never thought of him as *our* dog before.

I press my lips together and hold a finger to the corner of my mouth. "I'll keep that in mind and aim high. Negotiations will be tough, but I'll see what I can manage."

Percy's smile flattens. "Can you also manage a clean soul and freedom?"

I answer honestly, "If I could, I wouldn't be here."

"I used to understand everything. Or, at least, I think I understood everything. Now that I know that I don't know jack shit and that I'm aware that I don't know jack-shit?" He blows out a long breath. "It so much fucking worse."

"I know how that feels. I wish I could just understand why people hate. The science behind it and then I could fix it. Or I could try to fix it. All of my research and all I have is more questions. Like, why do they hate black people in particular?"

There's no answer he can give me that will justify or give reason to all of this. Nothing that will make me feel any better about what I saw in the hallway. Nothing that can quell the unease and unrest. Nothing that can counteract the large dose of fucking WOKE now coursing through my veins.

Percy raises his eyebrows. "That's not true," he replies,

I point to the swastika hanging above his bed. "That says otherwise."

He swings his legs to the end of the bed. "No, I mean the Reich doesn't just hate black people. They also hate the Jews, Hispanics, homosexuals, bisexuals, Jehovah's Witnesses, feminists…" He ticks the list off on his tattooed fingers. "Oh, yeah, and liberals."

"So, just like the Nazis then?" I ask, feeling a sickness in my stomach. Acid trying to purify the hatred I've been swallowing and ignoring for years.

He swipes at the corner of his lip with his thumb and leans on his elbows. "Nope. The Nazis were also against alcoholics. And I don't know if you've gotten a good look at the size of the bar at the gatherings lately, but you won't find too much opposition to that here. Nazis also murdered the mentally ill, and well, you can't exactly be sane to spout the shit that they do here." He looks to the floor and rubs his palm over his face. "I know I wasn't. I just wish I realized all this sooner, or never. This in-between shit is fucking killing me. But I was deaf to anything other than the hate ringing in my ears back then. That's for fucking sure."

"That's who you *were*," I tell him. "Albert Einstein once said, *The measure of intelligence is the ability to change*, and that's what you've done. What you're working on. Changing. I, myself, just realized what I've been passing off as witnessing and studying, is actually passive behavior. I've been standing by and watching all of this. The violence, the propaganda, the disgusting things said, without doing a damn thing about it. How does that make me any better?"

Percy scoffs. "Michaela, Not doing anything doesn't make you a racist asshole. You never terrorized black-owned businesses or got locked up for burning a Jewish-owned hardware store to the ground for no reason at all. I was a racist asshole. You were a pawn in our fathers' weird plans," he says, trying to relieve me of some of the guilt I can feel he's all too familiar with.

"So, were you," I point out.

He rolls his eyes as if it's not the same, even though we are both a product of manipulation. "Still, not doing anything don't make you a fucking racist. It don't make you one of them," he points out. He reaches for a pack of cigarettes and pulls one out with his teeth, tossing the pack back onto the nightstand. He leans back against the headboard and lights it, staring up at the symbol above his head as he takes a drag, then quickly looks away from the symbol that probably haunts him at night, one he can probably still see even though his eyes are shut tight. "You ain't ever been a bad person. I knew that when we were kids, and I know it now."

A thought occurs to me. A truth I can set free.

"There is a wrong I can right," I sit up and take a deep breath. "Pike isn't the one who ratted on you. Who got you locked away."

"I know," he says, his answer taking me by surprise.

He frowns. "After I got out of the joint, my old man was spewing his regular bullshit about Pike. The blame he placed on him for me catching so much time had only gotten worse. *Had* only gotten worse. Not only was Pike the one who ratted on me, but he's now the one responsible for my mother's death. At first, I bought it. I didn't think the old man would lie to me about some shit as serious as the person responsible for killin' my moms. I did some diggin' of my own. I asked some of the OG members who were around back then about my moms. Made them think I was just reminiscing about her. It turns out she ran away from this fucking place, from Darius, when I was seven. Darius always told me she was running from someone and left it at that. Never said it was him she was running from. I Googled her name and found the article. She died in a car accident shortly after she left."

"And you didn't buy it?" I ask.

Percy raises his eyebrows. "No, the old man is getting sloppy in his lies. Has been ever since your old man...well, you know. Pike's around my age, and he's a bad motherfucker, don't get me wrong, I know that, but even the baddest motherfuckers among us wasn't out on the streets murdering women for no fucking reason at all when they're in second grade. Even if he could have done it, Pike isn't that kind of guy. He was a dick to me, for sure, but I deserved it, and I respect that he lives by a code. He ain't no rat and won't ever be no rat. Besides, half of the shit I told him in juvie when I was running my mouth wasn't what came up in the FED's report. That was some inside shit that only a few people knew, but Pike, he wasn't one of them."

"Do you know who ratted?" I ask, sheepishly, needing to know exactly how much Percy knows and how much of a surprise what I'm about to tell him is going to be.

"Yeah, and it wasn't no rat." Percy chuckles. "Turns out, it was a mouse."

"A mouse?" I scrunch my nose.

He smiles. "A *Mickey* Mouse."

Shit.

"You knew?" I ask, leaping off the bed.

"Of course, I fucking did. You came to visit me in prison. You looked fucking terrified. I never saw you like that before. You were always so strong, so leveled-headed. You were on the other side of that fucking glass thing shaking like you were naked in a snow storm. I could see you didn't want to be there, and at first, I thought, *of course she doesn't want to be here, neither do I, it's fucking prison.* Not only that, but you asked me about all sorts of shit you would never have asked me about before. Matter of fact, we did more talking that day then we had since we were fucking kids."

Guilt creeps through my brain causing my body to go cold.

I slowly approach the bed and sit down again, nervously tugging at the hem of my shorts. "What I did, did it have anything to do with why my family is dead?"

Percy takes a drag of his cigarette. "No, Darius never knew it was you. I didn't tell him after I figured it out. He assumed it was Pike the whole time because Pike was transferred out of the detention center shortly after the FBI submitted their evidence to try me as an adult. And I knew, but you gotta know that even monsters have limits. I would never have touched you or your family. I would rather have rotted in that place than hurt you or your sisters. Your moms was cool as fuck, too, always bringing me that bread she made. What kind was it?" He snaps his fingers while he thinks.

"Banana bread," I offer.

"That's it. That was some good shit."

"Then, why?"

"Your father wanted out. That's why he was killed. Shit was getting violent, and that's something your pops never agreed to. Your old man wanted to build a brotherhood to study how loyalty is built outside of a family structure."

Learned Loyalty. An in-depth analysis of loyalty outside of the family structure.

It makes sense now. It was the title of one of my dad's papers. I remember reading it when I was about nine years old. "How do you know that?"

"I found it recently in a drawer in Darius's office. He's got a bunch of his shit in there."

"I know. I found them to," I admit.

"What the fuck did I tell you about poking around?" he says, raising his voice in frustration.

"I know. I know. I couldn't help it," I reply. "But, why are my father's journals in Darius's office in the first place?"

Percy shrugs. "My guess is that Darius raided your house and your father's possessions shortly after his death to get rid of any evidence that this was all just a fucking joke. Your dad was in it for the knowledge and Darius wanted an army for his drug operation. When your old man told Darius he wanted out, Darius made a big show of telling him that he was free to go and that he wished him the best of luck, but to Darius, it was a betrayal he couldn't live with. He wasn't about to let your father live with it either. He knew too much that could take it all down." His face falls. "I told him not to. I tried to warn you. I even went as far as to send men to the beach house to warn you, but it was already too late."

"But why kill my entire family?" I ask, my chest heavy. "All of us? Why not just my dad?"

"Collateral damage," I suppose. At least, I suspect that's how Darius sees things." Percy shakes his head. "He also wasn't supposed to tell you guys that this was an experiment, but he did. If he couldn't let your pops live with that knowledge, then he probably couldn't his family live with it either."

Collateral damage. My sisters and mother died because my dad took us with him instead of running alone. The thought makes me hate my father even more. "What about Gutter? What was he? That happened after you were released," I say, needing an explanation. Not just for myself, but for Pike.

Percy frowns, staring at his feet. "I didn't go that day with the rest of the group. I wasn't there when Gutter was killed. But, I knew what was going down. I knew an innocent man was going to die as revenge for killing my mom, back when I briefly believed that was true." He scratches his eyebrow with his hand holding his cigarette. "It sounds even more ridiculous that I'm about to say this aloud, but I thought that by not being there, not participating in it, it would somehow save me from the guilt of his death." He blows out a long plume of smoke. "It turns out that I didn't need to be the one to deal the deadly blow for Gutter's blood to show up on my hands." He takes another drag. His eyebrows knit together in a deep V. "Everything I've ever done has been for this cause…a cause that doesn't even fucking exist. It's as made up as that purple dinosaur in a kid's cartoon. A cause not meant to do anything but hurt, and in the end, I deserve to feel every bit of that guilt because I fed into it. I fed it to others!"

I want to say something that will make him feel better, so I search my memory, my research. "Guilt is a learned emotion. It's relation to past mistakes, and its existence when previously absent, suggest evolution. Progress. You learned what is right and wrong, and the guilt you feel is proof of your progress."

Percy scoffs. "Now, you're just making shit up."

"I don't make shit up, and I'll have you know that I don't

joke when it comes to psychological facts. These are finite facts. They can't be argued with." I say, triumphantly. "But guilt can also keep a person from having fulfilling relationships. It shows that you've made progress, but you won't be able to move on until you let it go. You're not a bad person anymore."

He looks at me with sad eyes. "Oh, yeah? Is that what you're doing? Letting go of the guilt so you can move on?"

I rub my hands up and down my arms, suddenly feeling a chill although it can't be less than eighty degrees in this room. "Just because I have the knowledge of how guilt works, it doesn't mean that I've made use of that knowledge as of yet."

He holds my gaze. "Answer something for me. What makes someone a good person?" he asks, slowly, curiously. "How do we fix this shit?"

"I have an idea or two," I admit with a small smile tugging at the corner of my mouth. "And it's never too late to try."

"What's going on in that brain of yours, Mickey Mouse?" Percy asks.

There's a knock at the door. "Come in," Percy shouts.

Rage walks in. The girl who placed the fake house arrest bracelet on my wrist at Pike's house.

My recruit.

Of course, it's her. Her looks alone could gain her access anywhere without much question. Beautiful and innocent-looking. You wouldn't know what actually lurks beneath all that blonde hair and tan, clear skin.

Rage's shiny ponytail is long and smooth, reaching her waist. her blue eyes are bright and yet dull all at the same time. Full lips and high cheekbones, she's a picture of real-life Barbie-doll perfection. She's wearing tiny white shorts and a bright pink crop top that reads "Feelin' cute, might cut you."

White bikini strings poke out from underneath, tied together at the nape of her neck.

Rage plops down her light blue cheerleading tote bag onto the bed and looks around the room with her nose scrunched up in disgust. "You have cobwebs," she points out. "Cobwebs are abandoned spider webs, collecting dust and holding the decaying carcasses of other insects. There's also rat droppings in the courtyard. Rats carry diseases, including but not limited to: hantavirus, leptospirosis, lymphocytic choriomeningitis, Tularemia, and Salmonella. Clean your shit, and get rid of the rodents before you even think about calling me next time. I didn't come here to be a vessel for the plague." She takes out a bottle of hand sanitizer from her bag and slathers it onto her hands before tossing it back in. She places her hands on her hips. "Okay?"

"Uh…okay," Percy says.

It's obvious to me now, when it wasn't the first time we met, although I was a little preoccupied with being held against my will and getting a bomb strapped to my leg than I was trying to figure out Rage's quirks.

"Now, I get it," I practically sing. "You're a germaphobe. And I'm thinking that in your case, it's a symptom of your obsessive-compulsive disorder."

"Accurate," Rage says, not looking even the least bit offended. "And I get that you're super book smart, but, like, to point out people's flaws because although you have a high IQ, you doubt your ability to truly understand or connect with people and therefore have to show them your big swinging dick of a brain in a faux polite way in order to make people understand that you're smart and therefore making them feel inferior and growing your gigantic dick brain that you tuck back in your pants, so you swing it at the next inferior mind you cross paths with?"

Percy laughs, and I shoot him a scathing look. *Backstabber.*

"I mean," he corrects, clearing his throat. "I wouldn't go that far, but she's not wrong either."

Unsure of what to say to defend myself, mostly because I'm not sure that she's entirely wrong, I stick my tongue out at Percy and go with the classic pout.

"So, this is the new recruit?" Darius drawls, entering the room. "Very nice," he says, appraising Rage with his eyes. "And what's your name?"

"Regina," she says with a smile. "Regina George."

It takes everything I have not to roll my eyes. Regina George is a character from the movie *Mean Girls.*

Darius extends his hand to Rage. She keeps the fake smile plastered across her face but takes a large step back. "Sorry, germaphobe. I don't shake hands, but I can give you a solute or a thumbs up as a replacement."

Darius laughs and focuses his eyes on her chest. "Well, done Michaela. Regina can help you get ready for tonight."

"Tonight?" Percy asks. "For the barbecue?"

Darius smiles, showing off his jagged chipped front tooth. "It's not going to be a barbecue, exactly."

"It's not?" I ask, cocking my head and wondering what Darius is hiding behind his mischievous, evil grin.

"No, I have something else planned for tonight," he announces. "You two have waited long enough. The Reich needs you. The members need to know that our leadership is solid and that the next generation is ready to take their rightful places at the head of the table when the time comes. Tonight, we solidify that leadership. Tonight, we join you two together and ensure the future of The Reich."

"Excuse you me?" Rage asks, with a hand on her hip.

Percy and I exchange glances. We don't have to ask what Darius means. We know exactly what he has planned for tonight. An event he's been talking about and planning for our entire lives.

Our wedding.

11

MICKEY

OUTSIDE IN THE COURTYARD, the breeze blows hot against my face. My skin feels tight like I've been wrapped in packaging tape.

The smell of burning wood and liquor mixes with the smell of the surrounding pine trees in what would make a gag-worthy cologne.

White satin from my simple slip dress clings to my damp thighs as I walk down the aisle, escorted by Hoppy, whose own sweat smells like vodka and potato chips as it drips from the crook of his arm, drenching mine.

Weddings in the Reich aren't legally binding, since the Reich doesn't believe in legal anything. However, they do believe in a medieval ritual about the wedding night that has my pulse racing and my stomach filled with dread as I hold Percy's clammy hands and prepare to recite false promises. I feel both numb and enraged, if that's even possible. I use every drop of anger flowing through my blood to fuel my purpose. Every word dripping from my mouth is said with reverence and sincerity that makes me nauseous and eager to see Darius' blood pooling at my feet. This is just a play. This isn't something that can't be undone, and yet it feels like a betrayal.

My stomach rolls.

Rage stands beside me, wearing the same pink shirt and white shorts she wore earlier in the day. Her duties tonight include reluctant bridesmaid and witness. She looks bored, checking her nails and shuffling from one foot to the other.

Darius is wearing a dark blue suit jacket, jeans and a big, shit-eating grin. When he asks if we are ready, he sounds as if he's asking us if we are ready for our coronation as the King and Queen of this shithole.

Percy and I nod and exchange knowing glances. Darius had shuffled him from the trailer earlier, and since then, we've had no time to talk about the ceremony or plan for what's to come.

Escape wasn't an option either. I'm sure that the reason why several high-ranking Reich members were trailing me and pulling me one way or another today was not because they wanted to help me with the dress and my bouquet, but because Darius wanted to ensure that tonight would go forward without a hitch and remind me that cold feet were not an option.

Percy recites his vows, and although I assumed he would act the part and be more enthusiastic, his voice is almost monotone. "I promise to hold order in my household and to be accountable for my wife. I promise to uphold the teachings of the Reich, and I vow to uphold the distinctions between races as our supreme being intended when he created the white man in his image."

I tune out in order to hold my shit together and prevent my hands from trembling in Percy's. The middle finger on my right-hand spasms, and Percy doesn't draw attention to it. He simply holds it tighter in order to still the tremors.

"Are you ready, Michaela?" Darius asks.

I nod and force a smile. Darius states the words I am to repeat, and I do so without cringing outwardly, but only because I've practiced not cringing. It took hours of reciting the words until they became empty ones and my food stopped threatening to make a reappearance.

The vows are based on the original creed of the Klanswomen used by the KKK and the women of the KKK otherwise known as the WKKK. The Fourth Reich broke off from them because the KKK recruited women in the 1920's by promoting this radical idea of female equality, and that was just too much for some of the men who generally didn't like anyone being equal to them. Boom. The Fourth Reich was born. Or non-aborted.

Either way, here we are.

"I believe in the American home and understand that I'm the vessel for my husband. The one who will carry our children and ensure our family and the future of the Reich."

Deep breath. No bile. So far, so good.

"I believe in the mission of the woman and my role in the Reich. I stand with my husband equally and therefore agree to submit myself to him and his knowledge for the benefit of our family and the benefit of the American republic and will dutifully fulfill my role as wife and servant."

"I promise to protect our institutions the Reich supports and the institution of a supreme white America."

After the last words leave my mouth, I bow my head. It

looks as if it's out of respect and being truly humbled, but in actuality, it's because the bile has risen and I'm trying not to spew all over my dress because puking at your wedding is an all too obvious sign that something isn't right. I've worked too fucking hard for my fragile system to give me away and give them reasons to ask questions I'm already trying to make answers up for just in case it comes to that.

I don't even hear the bullshit Darius finishes the ceremony with. By the time I'm sure I've willed everything back into my stomach where it belongs, I raise my head and Percy lifts my vail. He plants a quick kiss on my lips before stepping back and allowing the crowd to clap and holler as he tugs me down the aisle. I guess it's over. I'm both relieved and utterly terrified because the night is far from over.

I look to Percy who is shaking his father's hand and accepting a congratulatory pat on the back.

Whatever relief I'm feeling is short lived. Again, I swallow down the bile threatening to make its presence known in all too dramatic fashion.

Percy tugs me down the long line of people waiting to offer their congratulations. I'm numb as I accept them, responding to empty words with only a smile and a nod and the occasional *thank you*, too preoccupied with what's to come. The ceremony might be over, but the night is far from finished.

Because tonight is my wedding night.

꿍

RAGE DISAPPEARED SHORTLY AFTER THE CEREMONY, NO doubt to tell Pike what just took place. I feel even more nauseous at what his reaction is going to be as I enter Percy's trailer.

I'm glad my family isn't appearing to me right now because even ghosts shouldn't have to bear witness for what is about to happen in this room. The Ceremony, as it's called.

Summed up, it's a sick ritual where all future leaders of the Reich require witnesses to their union. In layman's terms, they want to watch us fuck.

I remove my dress and undergarments and lift the covers, shaking as I slide between the cool sheets. I tug them up to cover my naked body. I remember Pike's knife that's strapped to my leg. I remove it from my garter and tuck it under one of the pillows.

And I wait.

There're a thousand hornets stinging at my skin, puncturing every nerve I have as the door swings open. Darius enters first, draped in a white robe. His lined face is expressionless, but it's his dark eyes that are glistening with amusement as he looks me over approvingly.

I ignore the impulse to protectively lift my knees to my chest and instead sit straight on the bed, my back flush against the cool metal of the headboard.

The other elders follow him inside the trailer, taking their places around the bed. I nod to Darius in greeting, and he nods back, opening a small book in his hands.

"We are honored to witness the consummation of the future of the Fourth Reich and are here to ensure that the joining takes place which will produce the next generation of pure bloods and pure souls." Daruis closes the book and nods to the man I know as Eleven. He opens the door once again and in walks Percy with his hands folded in front of him and his eyes to the ground. He's wearing the same white robe as the elders. The door is closed behind him. The sound of the lock clicking in place causes my spine to jump. The only jumping I want to do right now is out of the fucking window.

"God has honored you with this gift of your chosen one. May you serve him and the fourth Reich well. May you fulfill your duties and carry out his will as only he intended."

I want to both vomit and cringe. God? Really? They're bringing God into their bullshit? Then again, what better authority to claim to have than someone you can't ask questions or demand the truth from.

Percy steps to the side of the bed, and Darius removes the robe from Percy's shoulders to reveal a very naked, tattooed body underneath.

Percy doesn't so much as look at me as he peels the covers back from my body, exposing me to the men in the room who lean over with interested, lust-filled eyes to catch a glimpse as he places his hands on my knees and spreads my legs.

I swallow hard, but I can't stop my body from shaking. I can't pretend that I'm not disgusted and afraid and even more angry as his chest grazes mine.

He's supposed to be on my side! Why did he agree to this? Say something, Percy! I silently shout.

He pulls the blanket over us and braces himself on his forearms, leaning down he whispers in my ear, "Don't worry. Trust me. Please."

"Go on," Darius demands, sounding both irritated and eager.

Percy slides his hand under the pillow and out of the corner of my eye I see him pull something from underneath, and at first, I think it's my knife, but I can still feel it beneath my head. He reaches down, and I assume he's adjusting himself because after a few seconds I can feel him positioned at my entrance, and I close my eyes. But no matter how tightly shut they are, it can't block out the feeling of him thrusting inside of me. I take a deep breath, and to my relief, it doesn't hurt even though my body wasn't anywhere close to being ready. "Trust me," Percy whispers again.

I want to trust him, but it's hard with all the nonconsensual sex going on.

"We will have to inspect before we leave you to continue," Daruis announces.

"Just hurry the fuck up, so I can fuck my new bride in peace," Percy grates. His words are crass, but the way he's looking at me when he says it makes him appear almost apologetic for being inside of me.

If Pike wasn't going to kill him before, he sure as shit is going to kill him now.

Darius slides the blanket off of us, and Percy leans back so Darius can have a full view of penetration.

I'm shaking as Darius nods and then claps approvingly. "We have consummation." The rest of the men clap as well, looking downright disappointed when Darius ushers them from the room as they hold their books over their crotches to hide their erections.

Percy tugs the blanket back over us and rests on his elbows beside my head. He isn't touching me anywhere except for where our bodies are connected.

This wasn't a consummation. This was an exhibition for a bunch of pervs. Although now that they are leaving, I have no idea what's going to happen.

What if he wants to continue? To finish?

"Congratulations," Daruis says as he leaves the trailer and shuts the door.

I'm about to reach for the knife under the pillow when

Percy grabs my wrist. "Hold on," he groans, pulling out from my body. He pushes his hand between our bodies once more and sits up on his knees.

And then he takes his penis off.

Wait, he's taking his penis off!

"What the fuck?" I gasp as he tosses what I realize is a flesh toned dildo to the side of the bed. He then reaches between his legs. His face twists in agony as he removes a long strip of flesh colored tape, freeing his actual penis which was tucked up between his legs. "God fucking damn it!" he cries out, falling beside me on the bed and covering himself with the blankets. "I knew it would hurt, but holy shit," he laughs as his eyes tear up from the pain. "It was fine until I saw you naked. I didn't think I'd even get fucking hard, but I'm a fucking guy and ahhhh…it hurt so much worse."

He sits beside me and covers himself with the blanket. His face is red, and his teeth are gnashed together.

"What the fuck just happened here?" I ask, pulling the covers over my naked body and sitting up.

"What happened was that a bunch of old pervs think I fucked my non-legal wife on the night of our forced fake-wedding," he groans and takes a deep breath. When his pain ebbs, he turns to me. "Sorry if I hurt you with that thing. It's the closest I could get to the real deal on such short notice."

His eyes point to the dildo.

"So, you didn't. We didn't." I sigh in relief and let my head rest against the headboard. The relief doesn't last long. I snap my head to look at Percy who is breathing hard with a similar grin of relief on his face.

"No, we didn't." he says, sitting up next to me.

"But, why?" I ask. "Why go through all of this trouble? Why not just do it for real?"

"Because you can't get someone to trust you just because you ask them to. Someone recently taught me that trust has to be earned." Percy smiles. "And because I wanted to prove to them, and maybe even myself, that I'm not the monster they want me to be. Not anymore."

"Thank you," I breathe, suddenly at a loss for words while trying to understand this new revelation and what it means.

"So, what now?" I finally ask after a few beats of silence between us.

The window slides open, and a dark shadowy hand reaches over the ledge. I reach for the knife.

Percy picks his robe on the floor, wrapping it around his body. "What happens now is entirely up to you."

"Who the hell is that?" I ask as large a man pulls himself over the ledge. I clamor to the far edge of the bed, clutching my knife and wondering why the hell Percy isn't as concerned about someone climbing in through the window of his trailer.

Percy smiles. "Consider this a wedding gift."

The light shines on the man's arm, a rusted handcuff around his wrist. Exhaling, I loosen my grip on my weapon.

"Pike," I gasp, relieved and grateful that he's here.

He's here.

"Why the hell are you here?" I ask. "I feel like I keep asking you that."

"Because you do keep asking me that," he replies. Pike rakes my naked body over with a dark gaze so heated I feel as if I'm melting. His nostrils flare, and I look down, realizing why. In my hurry to get away from the would-be intruder, the blankets are no longer covering me.

Pike lurches forward and yanks them up my body. I tuck them beneath my chin and he spins around to Percy, cracking his knuckles. "Did he hurt you?" he says between his teeth.

"No. He didn't. I mean, we didn't," I stammer.

He looks down at Percy, baring his teeth like a wild animal. "Understand this, if your cock ever gets that close to her again. If you ever look at her for more than a second, I'll rip your fucking cock off and feed it to the alley cats."

Percy raises his hand in surrender. "Understood, man. You're a better man than me. If another man got that close to my old lady, I'd— "

"Trying to give me ideas?"

"Uh, no." Percy ties the sash of his robe. "You didn't ask me if I was hurt."

Pike scoffs. "You hurt?" His voice laced with sarcasm.

"Fuck yeah, I am. That idea of yours worked great, but shit ain't going to be right with my dick for a long fucking time."

Pike smirks. "It'll feel a lot worse when I cut it off and let you bleed out."

"This was your idea," I say to Pike. It's not a question.

"I'll take that as my cue to leave." Percy heads to the door. "I'll go back out to the party and tell them you're resting after we—"

Pike growls deep in his throat, standing between me and Percy.

"After, you know, the thing," Percy backtracks. "Lock the door behind me."

"Percy, wait!" I raise up to my knees and push Pike aside so I can see Percy.

"Yeah?"

"Thank you. For everything." I look to Pike.

Percy's gaze shifts to the floor, obviously uncomfortable with the sentiment. "Uh, yeah. Well, it was all Pike's idea. I just sent him a message, and well, he's here now." He thinks for a moment and lifts his eyes to Pike. "I know me and you got issues that can't be healed. I accept that. But I've known Mickey since we were kids. We may not really be married, but she's as close to family as I got. I might have put down my gun, but if you hurt one fucking hair on her head, you best believe I'll be picking it back up."

12

MICKEY

PIKE IS BEYOND HANDSOME. From the depth of his eyes and full lips to his sharp square. His oak colored hair falls into his face as he looks me up and down, casually draping over his otherwise very serious features.

His tight, white t-shirt shows every ridge of muscle flexing beneath. His strong thighs cased in light denim don't hinder him from being almost graceful as he stalks toward me. He turns the metal cuffs around on his wrists.

"Are you okay?" he asks me again.

"I…I think so," I reply, fixated as he rotates the cuff over and over again. "So much has happened. I haven't had a moment to take a mental inventory." He squats down so we are at eye level and gently swings my legs over the side of the bed, resting his hands on my knees.

"But are you okay?" Pike asks again, searching my eyes for the truth, tenderly rubbing his thumbs over the skin above my knees right over the matching scars I received courtesy of a fall off my bike.

"You know, when I was younger, Papa never kissed our

boo-boos or held us when we cried. Instead, he'd break down the science of our injury and explain the healing process." I laugh without smiling. "Not exactly comforting words for a four-year-old who just fell off her bike."

Papa wasn't the comforting type, and at first glance, no one in their right mind would think Pike would be either. But he is. At least to me. He's comfort wrapped around a steel frame. With him, I feel safe. Free.

"What's got you making that face, Mic?" He pulls me against his chest, and I inhale deeply.

I shake my head. "Physically, I'm fine. Mentally...I'm thinking about my father. Even if this was my real wedding day, knowing what I know now about him, he still wouldn't be here, even if he were alive."

"He was a traitor. A liar," Pike points out. "Don't waste your thoughts on him. Plus, it wasn't your real wedding day." He grips my legs possessively.

"I know, and maybe, it's because his approval was a competition between me and my sisters. Maybe, it's because I always held out hope for the hug or those words of reassurance. But they never came, and although my disappointment mounted, my love for him never faded." I sniffle. "If anything, it only grew. But now, saying this aloud to you, I can finally hear myself, and knowing what he's done and why? I can't believe I didn't recognize it before. I can't believe I didn't see him for who he really is."

"Recognize what?" Pike asks, pushing a strand of hair from my eyes.

I lean into his touch. "Papa was a classic narcissist. The world revolved around him. *We* revolved around him. Him and his twisted goals. We were not his children. We were merely trophies on his shelf. He didn't comfort us because he didn't care. Not about us. Only himself."

"I couldn't even tell him if I had a bad day because he would just be irritated and blow me off as if my feelings were annoying."

"Do you know how hard I tried to make him love me? When the accomplishments weren't enough for anything more than a *great, what's next*? I rebelled. I got a D on a science project once."

Pike raises an eyebrow.

"I know, but trust me, to me and to my father, a D was the ultimate act of rebellion. It may not be as direct as breaking someone's jaw, but it hit him just as hard. But when I showed it to him, it only earned me the silent treatment from Papa. He didn't speak to me until my next test. So, I tried being honest with him. I opened up to him. I went into his office one night, and I told him that I love him, and I'd like to explain the way I've been feeling lately and wanted to talk to him about the pressure I'm under. I just wanted him to listen. To react. Something."

"What did he say?" Pike presses. He cups my face in his hand and I turn my head to brush my lips over his open palm.

"He shut me down. Rolled his eyes and told me that I was being emotional due to my overactive hormones. He dismissed my feelings with a diagnosis."

"It's like he couldn't handle even the most basic human emotion. I don't know if he just didn't want to talk about them or…or if he even had them. I tried to think of what could have happened to him to make him so cold, so unavailable, but that only caused me to lie awake at night and analyze him over and over again, when the truth is, I didn't have enough information to go on, and it's not like I could say, "Hey Papa, anything in your past ever happen that would make you this emotionally twisted person? Ever been spanked in public? Exposed to any sexual situations before puberty?" I shake my head. "I guess I'll always wonder."

"People are complicated," he offers. "You of all people should know that by now."

"They are so much more than complicated, and yet—" I look him in his beautiful eyes, "—sometimes, what we feel can be so simple."

"You mean like this shit between us?" Pike presses a kiss to the inside of my knee. "Because it's complicated as fuck, but what I'm feeling right now, for you. What I want. From you. " He scrapes his teeth up the inside of my thigh. "It's pretty fucking simple. It's all the other shit that comes with it that's hard."

He sits up on his knees and lightly wraps his hand around my throat. A possessive hold. "My mom left me, when I was a kid. I didn't get a chance to get to know if she was the caring kind or not but from what I remember, I think she could have been. She left me, Mic, but you can't. You can put distance between us, but you can't really leave."

"Because you'll always find me?" I swallow hard.

"No," He rubs his hand over his chest like he's in pain. "Because you're still in here. But when you're gone, this place inside of me…it hurts like fucking hell. Like I want to punch inside my own chest and tear my fucking heart out to stop the hurt." His grip on my throat grows tighter. "You still think I'm a psychopath?"

"Yes," I reply.

He grins.

"You still think I'm crazy?"

He bites my bottom lip. "Craziest bitch I've ever met."

Crazy and psycho. A love story.

"I think I've finally figured you out, Pike."

"I thought you already did that?" He dips his head, lightly brushing his lips over my collar bone.

My entire body tingles. Resting my hands on the mattress my head falls back to give him better access to my body. "No. I thought I had, but I was wrong. I saw simple observations and drew conclusions. I judged you, and I'm sorry for that. I wasn't even close. You're so much more than a man with a reading disorder. More than your loneliness. You're complicated. Strong. The strongest man I've ever known. You're loyal, and you'll fight for what's yours, even if it means your own life. I find comfort with you when I was never able to find comfort in my own father."

His voice is low and rough, vibrating against my skin. "Because you're mine."

I try to sit up but he pushes me back down. "I'm not—"

Pike cuts me off. "You're not mine like the shit in my pawn shop, Mic. But you're mine as much as I'm yours. A part of me. But like the shit in my shop, you were right about all of it. I was trying to fill a hole inside, but with you, there ain't no hole." He licks a trail down my belly button. "And I'd fucking die for you."

My entire body begins to tremble from the growing desire and from the idea that Pike believes I complete him. His words are both thrilling and terrifying. "I don't want you to make that sacrifice. Not for me."

"And I won't, because I won't die…" he looks up at me as he spreads my legs wide. He runs his nose through my wet folds. "But not because I'm not willing to."

His confession inspires me to lower the shield around my

heart to the possibility of a life with Pike. A real life. "What happens after this is all over?"

Pike crawls over my body, brushing his lips over mine. I shudder. "You and me. That's what's happens. Shit, it's already happened. There's no going back now, Mic."

I wish it were that easy. I think about my sister. About her recovery. About what life outside of these walls will look like for us.

"Mic," he says, looking up from where his mouth is presses against my chest above the swell of my breasts. "I can promise you this. After this shit is over, I'm taking you home."

Home.

The word rolls around in my brain and in my heart as Pike raises up to kiss the tears from my cheeks. "Let me show you, Mic. I'm not good with words the way you are. I can't explain how I feel, but I want to show you."

He kisses me hard, breathing me in. His tongue meets mine and our fingers tangle in one another's hair. After a minute, he pulls back. His eyes meet mine, posing both a question and a dare.

"Tell me you want me to show you," he rasps.

"Yes. Show me," I groan, throwing my head back and closing my eyes as Pike trails his lips across my neck and then down between my breasts. My nipples harden, and he moans as he takes one into his mouth. My back arches into his touch as he licks and sucks until my legs are kicking out beneath my body. He moves to my other nipple, and I rub my legs together, to create friction. Craving more of this. More of him. My thighs are slick with my own wetness as my body is assaulted and cherished in a way I never knew it could be.

He releases my nipple with a pop then presses me back against the bed. He's both tender and passionate as he licks his down way between my legs, which he tosses over his shoulders. I tug on his hair while he flattens his tongue against my clit, stroking and licking. Teasing and pleasing. The tension in my lower stomach grows and I feel like I'm being wound up from the inside like a spring being pushed into place.

My vision blurs as he uses one and then two fingers to penetrate me. His scruffy face rubs on the inside of my thighs. "I love the way you fucking taste," he moans against my clit.

What he's doing to me, for me, the licks the sucks the feeling he's creating inside of me, these are his words.

I arch up into his face, holding tight onto his hair. He growls and continues to devour me. I feel like I'm going to come, but the way he slows his tongue and the stroke of his finger is sweet agony, the way he brings me to the edge and then holds me there. The best agony.

Just like us. The best agony one can find in another human being.

"Come," he growls. He grazes his teeth over my clit, and I'm done, breaking apart under his master touch. His hand reaches up and covers my mouth, muting the sound of his name being screamed from my lips. I bite down on his finger and hold it between my teeth until I come back down.

I understand now. My heart swells. Pike understands me. Not just my body.

Me.

Tears pour from my eyes. Pike raises up and straddles my thighs with his muscular legs. He dips down to once more lick them away. I'm sobbing and clenching my legs around him, needing more of whatever this is that came through the floodgates when I opened up my heart to him. More of his feelings. His love.

His fucking cock deep inside of me.

"Did I hurt you?" he asks, looking down at me with lines creasing his forehead.

I sniffle. "Not in the way you think. I'm fine. I'm just taking this all in. You. Us." I scratch my fingernails over the scruff on his jaw and tuck his hair behind his ear. "I'm yours. I understand what you're trying to tell me, and you're right. I'm totally fucking yours."

"Say that a-fucking-gain." he orders, biting at my lip.

"I'm yours," I moan as his lips capture mine, and we speak in his language with our tongues, our mouths, our bodies.

"You need more?" Pike asks, sucking my bottom lip into his mouth, holding my jaw in his hand.

"Yes," I breathe. He scrapes his jaw against my cheek, and the friction causes me to squirm beneath him.

Pike growls and makes quick work of his jeans, pushing them to the floor, he lifts me off the bed and carries me to the other side of the room, pressing me up against the wall. His cock throbs between us. Moisture drips from the tip, wetting my stomach.

"Wrap your legs around me," he demands. I comply without question, wrapping my tight core around the hard muscle of his body and shaft.

"You like doing what you're told," he muses, teasing my pussy with the head of his thick cock.

I open my mouth to argue, but the words don't come out because he's right. In this context, I love doing what I'm told. I love the way he responds to my compliance.

I love that I trust him to do any and all of it.

"I want to take my time with you, but I know we can't, but I'm going to make the most of this. The most of you," he promises.

"Yes. Please," I beg.

His hands move to my ass, digging his fingers into my flesh. His lips find mine once more, teasing and licking along the seam. "You taste so fucking sweet."

I'm lost in his words. I open my mouth to the invasion of his tongue and savor the feeling of his against mine, of our bodies pressed so tightly together.

It's as if we are in our own bubble, and nothing can touch us here, and I never want to leave if it means leaving his arms, his warmth. He takes one hand off my ass to reach between us, pushing his fingers inside. The moment he reaches the wetness, pooling between my legs, I see stars.

"So fucking wet for me," he says against my jaw. His voice is raspy and dark. "Tell me what you want me to do to this beautiful body of yours. To this gorgeous pussy." He hooks his finger and strokes that magical spot within that makes me whimper and my body feel as if he's set it on fire.

My mouth can't seem to form words, but I manage a gasp when he strokes me harder. Faster. I cry out and tighten my legs around his waist. "I want you."

"What do you want me to do to you?"

"I…I want you to fuck me."

"I've never wanted to do anything more in my entire fucking life than fuck you right now." He unwraps my legs from his waist and sets me on the floor. He kneels to give my clit another slow, languid kiss that renders me unable to stand or see or even breathe.

"Fuck, Mic," he groans. He doesn't waste a minute, scooping me back up and setting me on top of the small dresser. My legs take the place they had before around his body. "Do you want me?" he asks, holding my gaze. It's a different way of phrasing what he's asked me before, but the way he asks doesn't hold the same meaning. There's something more within the question. A fragility I didn't expect. It's almost as if he's asking me if he's okay. If he's good enough.

I cup his face in my hands and stare deep into his green eyes. "Pike?"

"Yeah?" he asks, breathing hard, barely holding it together.

"Fuck me. Now."

With a groan and gritted teeth, he pushes inside me with enough force that I'm surprised we don't break the dresser or the wall. I'm not even part of the world anymore. The hateful, disappointing, disheartening, broken world. I'm part of Pike. We are one.

I'm being stretched impossibly open as he fills me with every inch of himself. He feels slick and hot as I pulse around his cock.

He pulls back and thrusts in harder, possessively, telling me more than any conversation anyone could have, it doesn't take me long to lose myself, both in mind and in body. "I want to feel you come around my cock. I want to feel you. All of you. Give it to me, Mic. Give me you."

I hold on for dear life while I'm consumed with the orgasm that wraps around me like I'm being strangled. I can't breathe, and just when I think I'm going to pass out, I'm hit with an explosion of pleasure that crashes into me over and over again. Pure bliss that spreads through my entire body before finally weaving its way around my heart. It's not just a mind-blowing orgasm that makes me forget time, space, science, hatred, loss. It's the kind that feeds your soul and heals your body.

It's love.

Pikes face is tight with tension. His neck chorded. His ab

muscles constrict. "Mic! Oh, fuck, Mic!" Pike comes with a loud groan. I feel his cock pulsing his release within me, and I gasp at the bolt of pleasure that sizzles through my body at the feeling.

I'm in awe of Pike, of his raw power and determination. Of the way he fucks me like he's a part of my body.

He drops his forehead to mine. "Did you understand what I was trying to tell you this time?"

I nod against him, catching my breath. "I heard every damn word."

"It's me and you. Always. Don't ever forget it. Don't ever doubt it."

"I thought you said you weren't good with words?" I chuckle.

His eyes are dark and serious. "I'm not."

"So, you're a liar, then?" I tease.

He shakes his head slowly from side to side. "No, Mic. I've just been denying the truth." Pike pushes the damp hair from my eyes. He presses a kiss to my sweaty forehead. "Until you opened my eyes."

PIKE

"Why do you wear these?" Mickey asks, turning around one of the broken cuffs I wear on each wrist. "You never told me."

"It's a reminder of where I've been. Where I never want to go back," I explain.

"Are these real cuffs?"

"These are the first handcuffs that were ever wrapped around my wrists when I was arrested for the first time. I think I was fifteen or sixteen at the time," I reply.

Mickey continues to mindlessly spin them around, her naked body pressed up against mine. Her softness against my hardness. It's the first time I've felt any sort of peace in years.

I prop myself up on my elbow, facing her on the bed. "You know, I've been having these crazy dreams since the night you left. Every night, I dream of the town, of Logan's Beach, but what it would have looked like before there were houses or people here. Barren, like it would be in a drought. Not a drop of green. Not a blade of grass. Just dust and dirt and dead trees as far as the eye can see, and then, I wake up, and I wonder what the fuck I'm eating before bed that's making me dreaming about fucking trees and dirt."

Mickey mirrors my position, facing me. "When I was working on my doctorate, I wrote a paper on dream analysis. It's not a perfect science, but some images reoccurred in enough subjects' dreams to be able to analyze them based on the subjects' current life and emotional status. From there we were able to determine and assign those images meaning. For example, a barren landscape often means dissatisfaction, in particular dissatisfaction with one's love life."

Her cheeks burn as she speaks, and I can't help wanting to lick the blush from them all over again.

She catches me staring then clears her throat and continues. "It can also represent needing someone who isn't there or wanting someone who doesn't want you back." Her eyes meet mine, and I pull her closer into my body, inhaling the smell of her shampoo and relishing the feel of her little body against mine, her perfect tits crushed up against my chest. "But, the last thing can't be true, because if the dream was about me... I've always wanted you back. I'll always want you back."

"God, you're fucking sexy when you're talking all your smart shit." I groan, and I press my lips to hers. What started as a kitchen fire I could put out with a safety blanket, has erupted into a fire that can't be contained. Fuck it, let the place burn around us. Mickey is in my arms, and her lips are on mine. The entire fucking world could burn down, and I would die content for the first time in my life.

I chuckle, and she pulls back, searching my face. "What's so funny?" she asks with an adorable grin.

"Nothing," I say, diving back into the kiss, parting her lips with my tongue until she's moaning into my mouth, making my cock stir back to life once again.

It is funny, though.

I've collected a lot of shit over the years, plastering the walls of the pawn shop with it, but now, I have something that truly completes me. When I have Mickey, I have everything. Content in the chaos she brings into my life.

"Do you love me?" Mickey asks. She then shakes her head and drops her face into her hand. "Nevermind. That was a stupid question. It just kind of came out."

I pull her hand from her eyes. "Look at me, Mic."

She slowly lifts her gaze to mine. "I'm not good with the whole love thing, but I have this feeling that I want to protect you and strangle you all at the same time, the same one that tells me that we're linked by an invisible rope that can't be cut. The one that brings with it a pain I've never felt when we ain't together."

She sucks in a deep breath. "That's a much better explanation than pheromones and hormones, and yeah, I think that's love."

I take one of the broken cuffs off my wrist and clink it around hers. "Then yeah, Mic. I fucking love you."

I'm so wrapped up in the moment that I almost forget what I wanted to give her. "Here," I offer, reaching to the floor I pick up my jeans and pull out a note from the pocket.

On it is a name and an address. "Tomorrow at noon. Don't be late."

"Who is this person?" she asks, reading the name on the note. "What is this for?"

"It's to help you with your plan." I tap a finger on the note. "If you want to take down Darius for good, this is who you need to talk to. It's his supplier. You are going to go there, and pitch them a deal. While you're there you're going to find out everything you can about Darius. Who knows, maybe you'll discover something we didn't know before. Something that can help take him down."

"You're not going with me?" she asks.

"I can't. I don't do business with them, The Reich does. And you're…"

"Part of The Reich," she finishes, her shoulders slumping.

I lift her chin. "You can do this, and you will. You're not one of them. Never were. Remember that. Besides, they are going to love the deal you're going to pitch them. Trust me."

"What kind of deal?" she asks, sitting up straight with her shoulders back once again. She cocks her head to the side, looking very much intrigued by this new possibility.

I kiss the corner of her lips. Her body arches toward me on instinct as my lips trail further down her beautiful body. The party is still raging downstairs. We have a little more time.

I chuckle at her response to my touch.

"The kind of deal they can't fucking refuse."

13

MICKEY

Meeting with a cartel boss, wait, cartel leader, cartel grand wizard, whatever they are called, meeting the leader of a drug cartel isn't exactly how I saw any part of this plan going.

But here, I fucking am.

The hotel is on the affluent side of town. The side that puts the 'beach' in Logan's Beach. It's not far from the townhouse my family used every summer. I wonder what has happened to that place since then and remind myself to take Mindy there when all of this is over and she's feeling up to it.

Pike told me before he left that Mindy is happy and getting healthier by the day. She spends all of her time hanging out with Thorne in the Pawn Shop and loves greeting the customers silently since her damaged voice box still hasn't recovered. I also remind myself to take her to see a specialist when all of this is over.

I'm eager to see it for myself. To see my sister smiling and very much healthy and alive. It's what fuels me through my fears regarding this meeting that's about to take place and pushes me forward. Because I'm not just doing this for myself anymore. I'm doing it for Pike, for Mindy, and even though I never thought I'd even think it before, for Percy.

I park down the street so the van isn't caught on the security cameras and sneak my way inside the towering hotel through the staff entrance, passing large washers and dryers, a kitchen bigger than I've ever seen before, stretching down an entire corridor the length of a football field. There're dozens of staff members in varying uniforms and chef's coats shouting at one another and rushing about. Pots and pans clamor. Bells ring. A rolling car whizzes by me, almost running over my foot. It's being pushed by a man who looks like a fireman who is running toward a raging blaze and not like a waiter with a cartful of room service trays.

I find the staff elevator. The doors are about to close, but I manage to run and turn sideways, fitting in just before they shut. I find myself standing next to a man in a tuxedo holding onto the handle of a three-tiered room service tray.

When the doors open at the ninth floor, I get out and find suite 720 at the very end of the hallway. The only room with a solid oak double door entrance. The entire hotel smells like lavender, vanilla, and fresh laundry. I inhale deeply before raising my knuckles to knock .

It opens before I have a chance and I stumble as I'm caught off guard. A man wearing a Hawaiian shirt with a gold front tooth waves me inside. "Señora Lovejoy, right this way," he says.

My heart races as I follow him through a spacious bright living room to a sitting area bigger than Pike's entire apartment.

The man extends his hand toward a set of closed doors

and opens them for me. I step inside, but he doesn't follow, shutting the doors behind me.

This room is even bigger. Decorated with a modern grey and white pallet with a touch of silver and light wood accents scattered over shiny white tables and cabinetry. Floor to ceiling windows bath the room in bright light with dark blue sheer curtains tied on each side of the wall.

There's a painting leaning up against the wall opposite two plush white chairs. A sheet is pushed over the top as if it's new and recently unwrapped. The image of a woman standing in the center of what appears to be a rocky battlefield catches my eye. I walk over and crouch down to inspect it further. The painting itself was created in varying shades of grey, green, and muted gold. The only pop of color is where the artist used white to create light where they would otherwise be done.

The woman appears to be a warrior with long flowing red hair. Her fitted armor is ornate, but laughable since it doesn't cover her shoulders or chest and has that Wonder Woman heart affect around her ample breasts. One arm is raised, pointing a massive sword toward the sky. There's a halo effect around her head as the clouds above her open up, bathing her in light. She's not just a warrior though, a large pair of white wings takes up the majority of the painting's background.

"Do you like it?" a feminine voice asks. "It called to me when I entered this suite. I bought it and I'll be taking it home with me to Miami. It was painted by a local artist here in Logan's Beach. A very talented young woman the artist is, don't you agree?"

A very beautiful woman with a clear complexion and perfectly tanned skin steps beside me. She, herself, is a work of art. Perfectly pressed white suit, French manicure, and waves of shiny black hair.

"Yes, it's beautiful," I agree, turning back to the painting. The more I look at it, the more detail I discover. "Although, I admit, I don't know much about art. I'm more of a facts and science kind of person, but my sister, Mindy, she's the artist in my family. All I know about art I learned from her. She would love it though. That I know for sure."

"Ah, I see," she tilts her head toward the painting. "Do you know who she is? This woman in the painting?"

"An angel of some sort?" I ask, referring to her wings.

"Do you know any of the stories of Nemesis, the Greek goddess of revenge?" She folds her hands together behind her back.

"I don't believe I do. The stories I read as a kid were mostly real stories. Case studies. Scientific papers."

"Ah, well, there are many stories about Nemesis. She liked to point out the arrogance of men. One such story is when she took a young man, Narcissus, to a fountain and showed him his reflection. He fell in love with his own image and couldn't leave the fountain. Eventually, he died there, alone." She looks at me.

"Sounds like my father," I mutter.

She laughs. "Mine, too."

I look at the mask covering Nemesis's eyes. "Why does she wear a blindfold?"

"Because, revenge is selfish and blind. She knows this as the truth even though it's the reason behind her very existence, but also, because men often see what they want to see, even if that means being blind to the truth. Revenge itself is selfish. Revenge for the sake of others? That's—"

"Love," I finish for her.

"Very good." She nods. "I knew that I would like you, Michaela Lovejoy."

The praise from this complete stranger makes me smile.

She flashes me a bright white smile encased in perfect red lips.

I'm the last person alive that anyone could ever consider a sexist. I'm a feminist, for fuck's sake, but I admit that I'm guilty of making my own assumptions about the person whose been supplying The Reich's drugs. I pictured a man a lot like Darius, but this woman is nothing like Darius. Her long eyelashes flutter as she walks over to an iPad on the table, swiping and tapping on it several times before looking back up. Her face is slightly rounded, giving the impression of youth while the intelligence and wisdom in her eyes and her perfect posture tells me she's probably more around her late thirties.

"Come here. I've been waiting for you," she says with a Spanish accent. "There is much more you want to discuss with me than art, no?" She pushes the iPad away just as a little boy runs into the room and throws himself against her.

"Mami, Didi hit me again!" he cries into her shoulder, wrapping his arms around her neck like a little, chubby-armed python.

She unlatches him and clasps his hands in hers. "You tell your sister that I said not to hit you, and I'll have words with her when I'm done with the lady, okay, Papi?"

The little boy looks over his shoulder at me and gives me a dismissive, bored look before turning back to his mother. "What does the gringa want?"

"That's what I need to find out, and the sooner you leave us to conduct our business, the sooner I can join you and tell your sister not to hit you anymore." She releases him, extracting him from her body, and taps a manicured finger to the tip of his nose. "Okay?"

The little boy can't be more than four or five, but when he jumps from her lap to leave, he pauses long enough to say, "I thought you weren't doing business with dirty, lying gringos anymore?"

"Go!" she says, shooing him with her hand.

I cover my mouth with my hand to hide my laughter.

She laughs and claps her hands together. "Kids," she says to me before refocusing on her son. "Yes, but I never said anything about gring*as*."

He shrugs and runs to a set of double doors. For a second, it looks as if he's about to collide with them, but at the last minute, they open as if by magic, and he scurries through without missing a beat. "Mami said to stop hitting me, Didi, and to stop being a puta."

The doors shut, and she turns back to me. "As I said, *kids*. Do you have any?"

I shake my head. "No, I don't. Honestly, I've had a lot going on in my life. I've never really thought about it."

She sits on one of the plush white chairs, crossing her legs at the ankles. She taps her nails on the table. "You know that I research everyone I grant a meeting with. And your background is quite impressive. A doctor, right? So, tell me. Why is a smart girl like you wrapped up in the bullshit underbelly of Logan's Beach?"

I could ask her the same but I'm in her house so I refrain.

I hold her gaze. "My father. He was one of the founding members of The Reich." I keep myself from grimacing at my own words.

"Ah." She wags her finger. "I remember him. Smart man, but still...a man." She gestures to a comfortable chair caddy corner to another. There's a small table between the chairs with a glass decanter and two crystal tumblers. "Am I not what you were expecting?" She picks up the decanter and pours two drinks before she sits.

I perch myself at the edge of the chair. "More like an unexpected surprise, but a good one."

She unbuttons the jacket of her suit and hands me a glass of the amber liquid. She leans back and crosses her legs once more, smiling at me over the crystal glass. "It's okay. I get it all of the time. Everyone expects someone in my position to be an old white man with a cock, and they are all just as surprised as you are to find a Latina, a woman, at the helm of such an empire."

"I didn't mean to be surprised. I'm actually kind of mad at myself for it," I admit.

She waves me off. "I would do the same. I got to this position through hard work and by killing my bastard of an ex-husband." She leans forward and hooks her finger for me to do the same. I do, and she looks around before whispering, "Do you know what I do when men think they can take advantage of me just because I am a woman?"

"What?" I whisper back, genuinely interested.

She leans back and chuckles, swirling the liquid around in her glass. "I show them who has the bigger dick. And just so you know, it's always me."

I think I like this woman. "I'll keep that in mind in the future." I like her, but I'm also kind of afraid of her. Maybe, that's why I like her. It seems to be a running theme with me. I'm also kind of scared of Pike half of the time.

"I am Carmen Rivadulla." She extends her hand.

"Pleasure to meet you," I accept her handshake, which is firm and steady. She never takes her eyes off mine as I answer. It's a power move. I can respect that. "Thank you for seeing me."

"So," she says, clapping her hands and setting down her glass. "What brings a beautiful young woman like you to see me? You don't look like the standard issue member of the Fourth Reich." She looks me over and pauses. "My guess is that is because you're not."

"You're right. I'm not. I'm here because I need your help."

"Is it boy troubles? Because I'll tell you now that I'm out of the killing because he broke your heart business. That was a one and done, and although my husband deserved it, it doesn't mean I'm going to make a habit out of it." She thinks for a second. "Unless the son of a bitch hit you or your child. For that, I can grant an exception."

I almost spit out my drink. I wait for a second to force it back down my throat so I won't spit it all over her suit that probably costs more than everything I own. Actually, it could be a suit from a thrift store and would still cost more than everything I own. I shake my head and set down my glass next to hers, being mindful to use the shell coaster. "No, no broken hearts here. Well, yes, I have a broken heart, but it's not relevant as to why I'm here. I'm here on business. I have a proposal for you."

She nods her head slowly looking slightly impressed. "I understand, but broken hearts are always relevant. They are the motivation behind everything we do. We cry, we eat, we breathe, we fuck, we kill. All in the name of love. So, tell me, is love the motivation behind what brought you to me today?"

If she were anyone else, I would deny or deflect, but the way she's looking at me as though she can not only see my thoughts, but has experienced everything I have been going through, is not something I want to fuck with. Not with someone as dangerous as her and not when the stakes are so damn high.

"My family died," I admit. "They were murdered." I grimace because even though this has been my truth and my life for years it still feels like a knife to my gut when I hear the words spoken aloud. "The man who killed them is currently one of your buyers, and I'd like to propose an alternative to selling to him."

"An alternative?" she asks, raising her eyebrows.

I take a deep breath. "I want you to cut him out."

She leans forward with her elbow on her knee. "Ah, now we get to the interesting part." She waves her hand. "Go on. Tell me more."

I lay it out for her clearly and precisely. "Darius Alban is the buyer. I propose you cut him off, and in exchange, I will bring you a new buyer, not for heroin but for MDMA. Double the quantity, almost triple the profits."

"Ah, Darius." She looks up at me, and for a second, I think I've lost her. "He used to be quite a man, but he's since become…how you say, a misguided prick." She picks up her glass and taps a perfectly manicured red fingernail against the rim. She twists her lips and looks to the glass before finally speaking. "I do not like that racist motherfucker as much as the next human being, but he is a large buyer and to drop him and run that risk, I would need at least four times the profit, triple the quantity."

"Done," I say, leaning back in my chair.

"Ahhhhh," she says, wagging a finger at me. "You did not lead with your best offer. I knew you were a smart one. I accept. Just know that if you do not pull through on your end of the bargain, that it will not end well for you."

"I'm aware," I tell her. I don't add that there's a possibility that it won't end well for me anyway. "And so is Pike."

"I realize now why he wanted to send you. He knew we

would get along. Good," she says, slapping her hands on her knees.

"Wait, he wanted to send me? I thought he said you wouldn't see him because he isn't a member of the Reich. Because you two have no business together."

"All of that is true, except I'm always accepting new proposals. I, too, was surprised when he said he was sending his woman instead, but I understood when he told me that this is personal for you and that you needed to handle this on your own. I like that in a woman. Take charge of your own destiny. Handle your own shit. You are much like me in that way." She takes a sip of her drink. "Now that the business is all done, tell me, before the wild wolves posing as my children barge in again, what, exactly, did Darius do to you for you to want to ruin him? Tell me the entire story. This, I will not negotiate."

"It's not—"

She holds up a hand. "Do not say that it is not relevant, because it is," she says. "Also, I like to know the reasons for why I'm crushing a man. It…" She wrinkles her nose. "How do you say…increases the pleasure."

I pick up my glass, take a swig, and because I have nothing to lose, I talk. But I don't just talk. I tell her everything.

Every. Fucking. Thing.

My family. Pike. Darius. Percy. My sister.

All of it.

"That sounds like Darius," she says, tapping her finger against her glass. "Although, when I first met him, he went by another name. He was another man completely. He didn't have this hate rotting in his gut. He was a businessman, like any other. He used The Reich as an excuse to form an army. A shadow over the real business at hand."

My heart thrums hard and fast within my chest. "What other name did he go by?" This is the other reason I came here today. Get info that could destroy Darius. I flex my fingers which are shaking in anticipation.

Carmen smiles and leans back in her chair. "That information will cost you an additional ten percent on the first shipment."

I smile back and mirror her position. "Done."

"Ha! Again, you impress me," she says. "Let me tell you all about this person you know as Darius…"

By the time I leave the hotel, I'm carrying with me a proverbial tank-full of informational fuel. Enough to set fire to Darius and burn down The Reich.

I find a payphone outside of the hotel and dial zero. "I'd like to place a collect call to Pike's Pawn in Logan's Beach."

The phone rings, and after a moment, there's an answer. "Pike's Pawn, this is Thorne. Yes, I'll accept the call." There's a pause as the line connects. "Mickey, is that you?"

"It's me. Is Pike there?" I turn to face the street with my back against the phone.

"Mickey! Hey, I was just thinking about you. Mindy is here with me, too." She pauses and laughs. "She says hi. But no, Pike's not here. He just stepped out. What's up?'

"Can you give him a message for me?" I ask, looking around to make sure that no one is watching me or listening.

"Yeah, of course. Go ahead."

I take a deep breath. "Tell him that I have what we need. The plan is a go."

14

PIKE

FOOTBALL PLAYERS GET themselves psyched up before a game by yelling in one another's faces or by imagining their competition drowning their dog. I psyche myself up with pain. My own pain. And for me, there's no better pain than a new tattoo. I remove the plastic wrap from my forearm and gaze down at the fresh ink of Mickey's name scrawled in elaborate script from the inside of my elbow to my wrist. A reminder of who I'm fighting for and what's at stake tonight.

The real thrill comes from not just being able to see this through, but knowing that after tonight, Mickey is coming home.

Checking the clock, I realize I only have a few hours. I check the security cameras before heading back up to my apartment to shower and make a few calls to make sure the final arrangements are in place. The bell rings above the door.

Turning around, I spot Jo Jo without her usual hat. Her long blonde hair is dirty and tangled. Her clothes are torn. She's only wearing one shoe. There's a fresh bruise forming on her cheek and another along her jaw.

"What the fuck happened?" I ask, rushing over to her.

"Yeah, I'm fine." She shrugs, trying to act tough, but her lip is quivering. Blood is caked at the corner of her mouth. "Betty's boyfriend roughed me up. Said I wasn't pulling my weight around the house." She looks up to me with sad, hope-filled eyes. "Pike, do you think I can stay here for a little while? Just until he cools down."

"No. You're not staying for a little while. You're staying. Period. You ain't going back there. Not to Betty's and not back into the fucking system. Not now. Not ever," I assure her as rage boils in my veins. "Thorne!" I bark.

Jo Jo jumps back, then smiles her apology at me when I'm the one who should be apologizing to her for scaring her.

Thorne runs in from the back room. "What's up, boss?" She spots Jo Jo and sets down her clipboard on the new glass case that's just arrived to replace the one I shattered.

"Bring Jo Jo upstairs. Give her some food, and set her up with the PlayStation," I order.

We exchange knowing glances. "Of course," she says with a smile hiding her obvious concern. "Where are you going?"

My jaw tightens. "To take care of some shit I should've taken care of a long fucking time ago."

"Just make sure you're back in time." She looks up at the clock above the counter.

I have three hours before Darius's birthday celebration is underway. Plenty of time to remind these fuckers that they messed with the wrong fucking kid.

Thorne ushers Jo Jo from the room. Before they hit the stairs, Jo Jo looks back at me with a sad smile. "Thanks, Pike."

"You'll never have to go back there," I repeat, needing her

to know that my promise is a real one and not one spoken out of rage.

I race to Jo Jo's foster parents' house and pull my truck into the center of the lawn. I enter without knocking and drag Betty's boyfriend out into the yard by his hair while Betty screams from the porch. "You do not fucking hit kids," I roar as I land my fist into his face. "You will never fucking touch her again!" I rain down punch after punch, going blind from rage, taking out everything from my childhood out on this terrible excuse for a fucking man.

When I finally come to, I find a pair of cuffs that aren't mine around my wrists, in a place that I've been before and recognize immediately.

The back of a squad car.

ᘓ

"YOU'RE FREE TO GO. YOUR SISTER SPRUNG YOU." THE officer says, opening the cell door.

My sister?

At first, I think that the officer is confused or that whoever is here lied to them and said they were my sister to gain access to me, but then, she appears at the end of the hallway, and the truth I wasn't able to see before this very moment becomes all too clear. It comes in the form of five foot, seven inches of piercings and bright orange hair.

My sister?

Thorne…is my sister.

Holy shit.

I don't know how I didn't see it before. The way she makes the same expressions I do. Her terrible temper. The reason for the fact that I've never once thought about trying to fuck her. Plus, I trusted her from the moment I met her when everyone else in my life has had to earn that trust. It's because I recognized and felt a familiarity with her from the very first moment, but I never understood that feeling until right the fuck now.

"You...it's true," I say, not able to form the right words. I have so many questions and can't pick the right one from my brain.

Thorne looks surprised and relieved, knowing exactly what I'm referring to without having to ask. She nods. "Yeah. It's true."

I place my hands on her shoulders and search her eyes that are the same color as mine. "Why didn't you...why haven't you told me?"

Her eyes gloss over. "You never asked?" She laughs nervously and sniffles.

"Seriously, Thorne. Why? How?"

"It doesn't matter," she says, shaking her head and stepping out of my hold.

I follow her out of the police station. "Like hell it doesn't," I argue

"That's not what I mean. It matters, but it doesn't matter right now. This conversation can wait. Right now, don't you have somewhere to be?"

I can't argue with her on that one. "We're having that conversation," I promise her, although it sounds more like a warning.

Thorne's smile is a sad one. "I know. And you should know that I'm holding you to that." But I hear something else. Something she's not saying, but I hear louder than her actual words.

Don't die tonight.

15

MICKEY

THE PLAN HAS BEEN DISCUSSED and gone over a million times, but a baseball-sized worry is rotting in my stomach as the party begins and the clock ticks on.

It's almost time.

To calm myself I shove my hand into my back pocket containing one of Pike's cuffs. Feeling the rusted metal against my fingertips renews my strength for what's to come.

However, all the preparation in the world can't prepare me for Darius taking the stage or what he says next. "Fellow members of The Order of The Fourth Reich, I have a very special guest for you, tonight," Darius announces.

Horror fills my guts as the girl I was trying to recruit, Emma, the one Pike gave money to and offered a job, steps to the side of Darius, looking to her feet and fidgeting with her hands.

Darius wraps an arm around her, pressing her against his side. "This is Emma. She told me some very interesting things earlier today." Darius' eyes find mine and gleam with understanding. Instantly, I know tonight isn't going to go on as planned. He raises his voice. "We have a traitor among us!"

Suddenly, my arms are pinned behind my back. I struggle and kick, but it's no use. I'm trapped. I blow the hair from my face and stare Darius in his hate-filled eyes as he steps off the stage and struts toward me. "I will give you credit, Michaela. You've hidden your betrayal quite well." He spits in my face.

I jerk my head to the side, attempting to wipe his poisonous drool from my temple. "Fuck you," I seethe.

My eyes land on Emma, who is frozen still on the stage. She glances up and mouths *I'm sorry* before rushing away. I can't blame the girl. Darius probably offered her something better than money and a job. After all, that's what he does. He manipulates. However, knowing her reasoning behind giving me up doesn't make this situation any better or any less deadly.

"What the fuck is all of this about?" Percy asks, parting the crowd and stepping to my side.

Darius is all too eager to fill him in. "It turns out that your wife here already belongs to another. That your marriage isn't pure just like her heart isn't pure."

Percy steps between me and Darius. "You don't know what the fuck you're talking about, old man" he says, crossing his arms over his chest.

"Young Emma told me that Mickey tried to recruit her, and then a man by the name of Pike, who owns the pawn shop in town, the same one where Mickey was held captive for weeks and then suddenly escaped from, intervened and told Emma to go. She watched them behind the gas station. It seems Mickey and Pike were quite...*familiar* with one another."

Percy rolls his eyes. "That's what the fuck this is about?" Percy asks with a laugh. "I already know all about that."

"You do?" Darius asks, raising an eyebrow.

"You think my wife does something I don't know about? You taught me better than that." Percy turns and looks at me then back to his father. The entire Reich is now gathered around us, watching the scene play out. "So, let her the fuck go," he grates.

"No. Not until you explain why I should," Darius replies, widening his stance and standing his ground.

Percy rolls his eyes. "She made Pike believe they were friends so she could escape, she told you as much. So, of course, he's going to be friendly toward her. She did what she had to do in order to survive. He made her let the girl go because she was in his territory. So, she did and brought you another one in her place. She's not a fucking traitor. She's just smart. Too bad you're not smart enough to recognize it."

I'm proud of Percy right now. He's using his father's own manipulation techniques and throwing it right back in his face.

"You believe that the same Pike who killed your mother is friends with a member of the Reich? Maybe, you should be asking if she's also making us believe she's one of us?"

Percy runs his hands down his face, stretching his cheeks. "You know, you're so fixated on trying to make everyone into a traitor." He steps forward, pointing an accusing finger at his father. "It makes me wonder why. Because the only people looking for faults in the people around them are the ones who are guilty of their own."

Darius lip twitches. "Watch it, boy, before you say something you're going to regret."

Percy turns, his back to his father and glares at Hoppy,

who's holding me. "Let her fucking go, Hop. That's my fucking wife. She holds a higher rank than you." The look in Percy's eyes leaves no question of his authority. "Now."

Hoppy releases me and steps back.

I stretch my arms and my right shoulder painfully pops back into place. "Ahh," I moan, bending at the waist.

Percy kneels beside me. "Hopefully, we've dodged that fucking bullet," he whispers.

I stand back up and wrap my arms around him. I whisper in his ear, "Yes, we dodged that bullet. The question is, how many rounds are in his gun?"

There's a commotion by the stage. I release Percy, and we make our way to the front of the crowd. Two of the Reich's masked guards appear, with another trailing behind him. They're dragging something between them. I stand on my tip-toes to get a better look. No, it's a someone, not a something, and whoever it is...he's unconscious.

The guards turn the man toward us, and my heart stops.

It's Pike.

I withhold a gasp as my entire body screams to run to him. To save him.

"Speak of the fucking devil," Darius sings, strutting up to the stage. He lifts Pike's head by his hair. Blood drips from his nose and ear.

"We found him circling the perimeter, sir. We didn't see anyone else. Clocked him over the head pretty good," one of the guards says.

Darius claps his hands together in delight. "Well, tonight just got a whole lot more interesting."

"I knew he was coming," Percy tells his father. "I made him believe we were discussing the terms of the truce." He steps up onto the stage, and Darius releases Pike's hair. His chin falls to his chest just as my heart falls into my stomach. "He's a gift. From Mickey and myself. For you. To thank you for all you've done for us. Almost spoiled it there for a minute with your bullshit, but we're willing to overlook that. Even the best leaders among us have their flaws."

Darius smiles, but I can see him grinding his teeth while he glares at his son for speaking to him in such a way in front of his people.

This wasn't part of the plan. What are you up to, Percy?

Darius's eyes light up, and I'm not sure if it's for show or because he's genuinely thrilled with our 'gift.' "Well done, son," he says, without offering me any sort of apology. Then again, he could be facing an arsenal of weapons pointed at his bald head, and he still couldn't muster an apology. Like my father, he's a narcissist. It's not his fault. It's the fault of others or circumstance that made him do or say the things he does and says.

It's bullshit is what it is.

"There's more," I offer, deciding to move forward with my part of the plan. What more do I have to lose? Besides, it's not like I'm going to get another opportunity. "Have a seat," I point to Darius's makeshift throne. A large, wooden rocking chair nailed to the stage that doesn't actually rock. The three hooded guards drag Pike to the side of the stage to make room for us, and it takes a lot of willpower not to watch him as they go. I take my place beside Percy who gives me a curt nod.

"It's fucking go time," he whispers.

I take the folded paper from my back pocket. The one Nine found for us based on the information Carmen had given me. I clear my throat. "Tonight, we celebrate Darius's fiftieth birthday." The crowd claps, and Darius waves back like the fucking prom queen he is. "Darius has been our leader for a long time. He started the Fourth Reich thirty years ago along with my father. Recently, I found out that my father was a traitor to The Reich."

The audience gasps and whispers.

Darius furrows his brows, probably wondering where the hell I'm going with this.

Luckily, he won't have to wait long.

I continue. "And Darius was right. There are those among us who are false in their beliefs in the Reich and its message. Those who wish to bring it, bring *us*, down."

The whispers grow louder. Darius's eyes widen in anticipation of someone's head on a spike. Percy shushes the crowd, then nods to me to keep going. "I have, here, a birth certificate for someone in the Reich. Someone who isn't who they claim to be." I turn and look at Darius. The excitement in his eyes fades to fear.

I jerk my chin to Percy who takes out his phone. I breathe a silent sigh of relief that he's moving forward with the plan after all, even though I still have no idea why Pike is here or if he's okay. I shake my head of the thought and press on.

The backdrop of the stage lights up as the projector mounted above the clock of the warehouse shines upon it. "You'll see that this image is of a young Jewish boy at his bar mitzvah." The crowd boos. Percy clicks to the next slide. "This is an image of that same boy as a young man at his first school dance. His date is Alexa Brown, a young black woman. A woman who later married, then divorced that young man." The slide clicks again, and it's an image of the birth certificate I'm holding. "This is the birth certificate of that same young man. David Abramson." Percy clicks it again, and I see Darius go stiff in the corner of my eye. If I wasn't so terrified, I'd probably laugh. "You'll see here a name change form filed in the county clerk's office over thirty years ago when David Abramson officially changed his name." I turn and look Darius directly in his terrified, angry eyes. "To Darius Alban."

The crowd erupts. Darius leaps to his feet. "No, this isn't true. She's lying! She's the traitor!" Darius pulls a gun and descends on me. Before I know it, I'm on the ground, the barrel of his gun pressed against the nape of my neck.

The wind is knocked from my lungs, and I can't pull any air in because of the pressure of Darius's weight pressing me into the ground. He smacks the back of my head with the barrel of his gun, and I'm so dizzy that I vomit into my mouth and into the dirt, sucking it into my nose. I choke and cough.

Darius again presses the gun to my head. "I should have done this a long fucking time ago," he whispers in my ear.

"Get the fuck off of her!" Percy screams.

"You. You were in on this?" Darius grates. He turns to the crowd who is standing around us in shock as they witness the fall of their leader. "You think this is true? These are lies. Lies so that my son can take power before he's ready."

Percy scoffs. "I don't want the fucking throne. I want out. Away from all of this, and away from you." He's goading him, and I know why. He's trying to draw Darius's attention away from me.

He glares at Percy. "No. You're just weak. She's made you weak!" He emphasizes the comment with a press of the gun to my head. His other hand is pressing my cheek into the dirt. "And now, I'm going to remove that weakness from your life. For good."

On instinct, I blink away the blur and look for Pike. If I'm going to die, I want to see him one last time. Suddenly, he stands up. I blink again because what I'm seeing can't be real. But it is. He's standing, and his arms are free because…they were never bound to begin with. The guards remove their masks, revealing their faces. They aren't guards, at all. They aren't even members of the Reich.

I know this for certain because I know those faces, and they belong to none other than Nine, King, and Preppy.

Pike rushes Darius, who doesn't see him coming. I suck in a long breath of air the second Pike tackles him, tossing him from my back. Darius lands on his back but Pike grabs a hold of Darius's shirt and flips him over, pressing his fist against Darius's chest. Pike removes his own gun from the waistband of his pants and shoves the barrel into Darius's mouth. I roll over, coughing up mud and my own vomit. My vision begins to clear with every breath I take. I push up to my knees and watch Darius's eyes grow wide with fear and disbelief.

His lips move, and his words are mumbled as he tries to speak around the gun in his mouth.

"You've said enough in this lifetime. Now, all that's left to figure out is who is going to send you out of it," Pike seethes, his chest rising and falling with his restrained anger.

Pike looks over to me. "He's yours, Mic. If you want him," he offers. "I'm not giving you this. This is yours to take. Your choice. Does he die by my hand or yours? Either way?" Pike glares at Darius. "He's going to fucking die."

Darius screams and tries to kick his feet.

Nine, King, and Preppy step out in front of Pike, holding their guns on the crowd in case any of them decide to leap to Darius's defense. None of them do.

"Do it!" Someone shouts from the back of the crowd.

"Fuck, I'll do it!"

I look over my shoulder to find the owner of the last voice. Surprisingly, it's Hoppy. He shrugs. "What? I'm pretty sure he had my brother killed. Plus, he wouldn't give me his Netflix password."

I glance back at Pike who's still waiting for an answer.

The sentiment is almost sweet, considering he's asking if I want to kill a man or let him. As much as I've yearned for this moment, imagined it a million times over, I never imagined I'd also be with the man I love. Things have changed. I've changed, and so has my purpose. I don't want to hate those who hate.

I want to heal.

Everyone except Darius, that is.

I shake my head. "No, you were right. I can't come back from that."

Pike blows out a breath, looking relieved. "Good. Because I've already been there, so his death is nothing but a notch on my belt and a reason to fucking smile at night." He fingers the trigger.

"No, wait," Percy shouts.

Pike looks up. His nostrils flare. "We had a fucking deal."

"I know, and I get it. I'm just asking you to wait before this gets worse."

Preppy blurts out a burst of laughter. "It ain't going to get much worse for Darius," he points out.

"I mean for you," Percy says, sounding sincere.

"What is going on, Percy?" I ask, groaning as I'm finally able to get to my feet. I sway, but manage to stay upright. "Why wait? What aren't you telling us?"

"What the fuck does that mean," Pike grates. Nine, King, and Preppy move to stand between Percy and Pike.

Percy raises his hands. "I'm unarmed. And he deserves to die. There's no doubt about it. Just wait."

"How fucking long?" King asks, pointing his gun at Percy.

"Why?" Nine asks at the same time.

Blue and red lights flood the compound, circling around the courtyard. Men in all black gear, holding military-grade weapons descend upon the crowd who runs and screams, scattering like roaches in the light.

Pike releases his hold on Darius and sheathes his gun.

His friends do the same.

"This is why," Percy shouts over the sirens and commotion.

"You!" Darius accuses, staring up at his son from the ground. He raises himself up on his arms. "You did this!"

Pike rushes to my side, shielding me from the chaos. He nods to his friends who quietly slip away. I spot Rage's blond ponytail sitting in the field next to the compound holding something in her hand.

"No, you did this, old man" Percy retorts as the crowd is corralled by the swarming FBI agents. He looks around and holds out his arms. "This? This is all a fucking farce!" Percy wipes the back of his hand over the Fourth Reich tattoo on his neck, smearing the ink and revealing scarred, yet tattoo-free skin underneath. "You want to know how I got out of prison early?" He points to the agents surrounding us. "Well, now you fucking know. You've got a new rat to hate now."

"No. It can't be. Not you." Darius's jaw drops. He blinks through his confusion as if he could change what he's seeing before his eyes. "Of all the fucking people." His face reddens as he bares his teeth. "You!"

Percy nods, folding his hands in front of him in a prayer-like position. "Yeah, it was me. What? You really think I got out because of something you did?" He unfolds his hands and points an accusing finger at Darius. "Please. You were more concerned about getting revenge on who put me in prison than getting me out." He looks over his shoulder to Pike. "But Pike? He wasn't the rat, and even if he was, he still wouldn't be the one who got me locked up. We both know he had nothing to do with Mom's death. You wanted to clear out your competition, and you made up a reason, a scapegoat, for me to direct all the hate you taught me."

"Then, if not Pike, who ratted on you?" Darius asks, confusion lining his angry face as the officers tug his arms together and slap him in cuffs.

"You're still on that? You can't see the bigger fucking picture here?" Percy asks, in angry amazement.

Darius can't hear him over the noise in his head. "Who got you locked up? Who, damnit? Tell me!"

Percy smirks. "It was me. I got myself locked up. I did the things that I did, and I take responsibility for them, but I never would have done any of it if it weren't for you. You tainted my blood with hate. You made me fearful of what's different. You taught me to be violent and…" He trails off, shaking off images of the past with a jerk of his head. He looks to the sky and bites down on his bottom lip before refocusing his attention on Darius, who's now being dragged backward towards a squad car, digging his heels into the dirt as if he could prevent the inevitable. "I took responsibility for what I've done. Now, it's time you to do the same."

"Did that little bitch make you do this? Of course, she did. She's a fucking traitor, just like her old man. I'll kill her like I killed him. Like I killed her entire fucking family. I'll never forgive you for this! Any of you!" Darius roars, attempting to pull free from the officers, to no use. "You'll all rot in hell!"

"You first," Pike replies.

Percy steps up to his restrained father. "Nobody made me do anything, except you. And nobody will make me do anything anymore. And I don't need your forgiveness. The only person who needs to forgive me is *me*. And this is the first step toward that." The officers shove Darius inside the back of a blacked-out patrol car. "You are the one who started all of this, old man, but I'm the one whose ending it." Percy glances at me and then Pike. "With some help, of course."

"Noooo! This can't be happening. This won't happen. I won't let it. I won't let—" Darius cries are muted by the slam of the door.

Percy watches the patrol car as it disappears down the road. "Bye, *Dad*," he whispers, then spits on the ground, kicking dirt onto it with his boot. The rest of the agents shove random resisters into their various vehicles, and without a word, one by one, they take off into the night, leaving us standing there in the center of the courtyard, untouched and alone.

Percy turns around to face us. He looks to Pike. "We all good now?"

Pike nods. "That last part was a surprise. Never took you for a rat."

Percy shrugs, "Rats spread disease. That was Darius. All I spread was the truth. And a death sentence? That's what the old man would have done. I'm trying to be different, better." He holds out his hand. "So, again, I'll ask: we good now?"

"A deal is a deal," Pike says with a curt nod. He takes his hand and surprises me when the two do that bro thing half hug back tap thing that guys are so good at.

"What the hell is going on?" I ask, jerking my head between Pike and Percy. "You two really know how to piss a girl off by keeping her in the dark. Out with it. Now!"

"Your man and I made an agreement. He held up his end, and now, it's time for me to hold up mine. I'll be out of town by sun up." Percy looks at me. "I'm sorry, Mickey. For everything. For…all of it."

The sincerity in his voice reaches me loud and clear. "You righted a wrong. Something I've been trying to do myself," I say. "I forgive you."

"Thank you," he says, with glistening eyes. He takes a rag from his back pocket and wipes at the temporary ink covering his face and neck, revealing a less hateful-looking man underneath. He walks past us into the warehouse and grabs a duffel bag hidden behind a gasoline can. He drapes it over his shoulder and heads for his truck. As he passes Pike, he stops and looks us both over one last time. "Pike, take care of her. I meant what I said before. Don't you fucking hurt her."

Pike nods and tucks my hand into his in a reassuring gesture. "That you don't gotta fucking worry about. Ever."

My chest tightens along with my fingers around Pike's.

"What are you going to do now?" I call after Percy who tosses his duffel bag into the back of his truck. He opens the door and stands on the step. He takes a deep breath and smiles as if smelling the salty-pine air for the very first time. "I'm gonna go get my girl."

Percy drives off, and I think it's just me and Pike until Rage saunters over from the field. "Guess I won't be needing this," she says, tossing Pike a small remote. She tosses her own duffle bag over her shoulder and saunters over to a baby blue Vespa, her blonde ponytail swaying along the way. She takes off, the humming of her scooter fading as she disappears down the dirt path in the center of the field.

Pike takes my hand, and we begin to walk away, but I stop, removing my hand from his.

"What's wrong?" he asks.

I turn around and take one last look at the compound. I

can still hear the hateful chants that were repeated here. Ghostly words whispering all around me. "Is there anyone left inside?" I ask.

Pike shakes his head. "No, the FEDS cleared it."

I smile. "Good." I reach over and pluck the remote from his hands.

"What are you—"

I press the button, and the building explodes in a fiery ball of flames and smoke. The wind blows back my hair, and my face heats under the intensity.

"We have to go," Pike orders, pulling me through the field to his truck.

"What's wrong?" I ask, still basking in the glow of the explosion as we get inside.

"Nothing is wrong. I just have to get you home. Now." He throws the truck in reverse and speeds through the tall grass to the back road. His gaze meets mine as he spins the wheel, turning us around.

"Why?"

He reaches over and takes my hand pressing the back of it to his lips. "Because that was amazing, and because I've never been so fucking hard in my entire fucking life."

16

PIKE

"Where is she? Where's Mindy?" Mickey excitedly asks Thorne as we burst through the front door of the pawn shop. It's late, and Thorne looks exhausted but perks up when she sees us. Her shoulders lift as the weight of her worry disappears.

"Nice to see you, too," Thorne replies.

"Hey, sis," I greet.

"You know!" Mickey says, happily clapping her hands together.

"Wait, you knew?" I ask.

Mickey bites her bottom lip.

Thorne laughs. "Yeah, it took her a few days. Only several years less than it took you."

"Jo Jo?" I ask.

She points to the office. "She noticed that I was waiting up for you so she crashed in your office. Last time I checked, she was asleep on your desk."

"Thank you. For everything," I tell her.

Mickey frowns. "I'm so happy to see you, Thorne, but

seriously, where is Mindy?" She bounces on the balls of her feet, her eyes wild with excitement.

Thorne points up the stairs, and Mickey wastes no time bounding up two a time.

"You two can…uh…catch up. It's been a late night, so I'll just crash on the cot next to Jo Jo so you don't have to worry about her."

I put my arm around Thorne, and she yelps in surprise as I pull her into my chest for a long overdue hug.

"At least, you smell better this time." She sniffs my shirt. "But why do you smell like a fire?"

"More like an explosion," I correct.

She pulls away from me and opens her mouth before shutting it again. "You know, I am really tired so whatever weird tale that is, you're going to have to save it for tomorrow." She joins Jo Jo in the office, and I head up the stairs to find Mickey.

I'm loving how enthusiastic Mickey is right now. Most people in her position would just want a shower and a nap. I laugh to myself and watch her burst through my apartment door. She's probably still high from all of the adrenaline. Explosions have a way of doing that to people.

"You kept her in the cage!" Mickey yells, running to the corner of the room. She drops to her knees. "How could you do that to her?"

"I kept the door open," I reply. "Sorry, I didn't realize you were so against it."

A sinking feeling begins in the pit of my stomach. A spark of worry that pulls at the hairs at the back of my neck, plucking at them one by one.

Mickey's shaking as she reaches inside of the cage. When she pulls back out, she sits cross-legged on the floor with her back to me. "It's okay now. I'm here. We're together again. I love you. I'm never leaving you again. I'm so happy that you're alive." She continues to whisper while rocking back and forth.

"Mic?" I ask, taking tentative steps over to her, wondering what I'm missing. What the cause could be for this reaction. I'm not heartless. I knew she'd be happy, but this seems a bit much given the situation.

Mickey looks over her shoulder. Her eyes are wide and wild, but not with excitement, but the same dull focus they had the night I found her wandering down the road.

I freeze. My chest seizes.

Shit.

"Thank you," Mickey says, a tear spilling down her cheek. "For giving me Mindy back. For protecting her."

The sinking feeling turns into all out dread.

I stagger backward, and when I hit the wall I drop to my ass.

Mickey is still smiling at me, but it doesn't reach her eyes because as much as I don't want to admit it, Mickey isn't in there anymore. What's left is a confused shadow of the girl who just took on the entire Fourth Reich without showing even a hint of fear.

And then shattered.

Mickey spins around on the ground, revealing the dark ball of fur on her lap. She lifts her arms, hugging the squirming puppy tighter, pressing her cheek against its head.

"My sister thanks you, too."

ဢ

My head is spinning, and my heart is racing. I head downstairs, leaving Mickey in my apartment with the puppy.

I run into Thorne. "Hey," she says with a bright smile that quickly falls when she sees the expression on my face. "What the fuck is wrong? What happened?"

I say nothing because I have no clue what fucking words to use.

"Tell me, Pike! What the fuck happened? Where's Mickey?" She looks around.

I stare at the broken case. "She's upstairs, and no, it's not okay." I close my eyes tightly. "Nothing is fucking okay."

Thorne cautiously approaches me. "Hey, tell me."

"She broke," I say, meeting her eyes. "It was all too much, and it fucking broke her, and I don't know where to go from here." I point to the stairs. "She's up there right now rocking the fucking dog thinking it's her dead sister, Mindy." I shake my head. "I can't believe I thought she was talking about the dog the entire time. That she named it Mindy. This…this wasn't anything I fucking saw coming." Anger and guilt tug at my heart. "I knew she saw things from time to time, but she always explained it as a coping mechanism. She always knew they weren't real. This…this is different."

Thorne looks like I've just punched her in the fucking gut. She wraps a hand around her throat and the other around her midsection. "I'm so sorry." She pulls back with glistening eyes. "Any idea what you're going to do?"

I shake my head. "Not a fucking clue."

"What do you want me to do? Do you want me to go upstairs and keep an eye on Mickey?" She sniffles. "Give you some time to think things through?"

I nod and rub my hands over my face. "Yeah, thanks, sis."

She bites her lip and heads up the stairs.

Gutter would be the person I'd call to find out what the best thing to do for Mickey would be, but he's fucking dead.

As dead as the look in Mickey's eyes.

I grab the first thing my hand lands on, a gold bowling trophy, and launch it across the room with everything I have. It crashes into a glass case, bursting it open, glass shattering everywhere.

The sound of my own scream is all I can hear until a tap on my shoulder has me spinning around, startled.

Thorne is standing there with a frightened look on her face, but I realize it's not me she's afraid of. It's what she's reluctant to say.

"Just say it," I spit.

She bits her lip and nervously twirls the bead dangling at the end of her belly-ring. "I went upstairs to find Mickey, but…she's gone. So, is the dog."

17

PIKE

BY THE TIME the sun begins to rise, I've run out of places to look for Mickey.

My phone rings. It's Thorne.

"Any luck?" she asks, sounding almost as anxious as I am.

"No," I reply, slamming my hand against the steering wheel.

I pass the *Welcome to Logan's Beach* sign where I found Mickey that first night. A thought occurs to me. One last place she could be.

Yanking on the wheel, I turn the truck around, bumping over the median. I head in the direction of the causeway, toward the beach. It's literally the last place I think she'd go, and yet it's exactly where I'm hoping to find her.

I pull up to the boarded-up beach house and get out of the truck. The one she spent summers with her family in. Where I took her the night I found her on the road.

Please be here.

I don't hear or see any signs of life. Even the seagulls

aren't out and about this early. The sounds of the crashing waves and the bristling of the palm fronds are the only sounds in the salty air.

"Mickey?" I call out, rounding the building to the beach.

The puppy comes barreling over to me, crashing into my legs. I lift it in my arms and scratch its neck. "Where is she, girl?"

I find Mickey sitting in the sand facing the water. The rising tide splashes around her body, sinking her body into the wet sand. Her dark hair is blowing all around her, and other than the slight rising and falling of her shoulders, she's completely still.

"Mic?" I ask, setting the puppy down.

The puppy jumps onto her lap, and when she doesn't get any sort of reaction from Mickey, she jumps into the sand. When her paws hit the water, she leaps like a cat back into the dry sand, curling up in a ball behind Mickey's back.

"Mic?" I ask again, standing beside her.

She's staring off into the distance, tear stains on her pale cheeks.

"I don't know what's real and what's not anymore," she finally says.

"I'm real," I tell her, my fucking windpipe closing in on itself. I clear my throat. "I'm very fucking real."

She looks up at me. Her eyes are no longer dead but sad and confused. I sit down beside her in the wet sand, and she rests her head on my shoulder, pressing her palm to my chest. "I know you're real," she says, her cheeks stained with her tears. "You are my constant." She releases a shaky sigh. "The rest of the world, everything I see, everything else…it's all just variables."

She presses a soft kiss to the side of my mouth. "Please, I need you. I need you to show me that you're still real," she begs.

My mind thinks it's a terrible idea, but she's already hurting so much, and with that one kiss, my body doesn't care what else is going on. My heart breaks even more as she steps back and tears off her shirt and strips off her shorts, standing there naked and vulnerable in front of me. "Please," she says once more, and my control is lost. I scoop her up in my arms and set her down on the counter. I want to make her feel good. Maybe, for the last time in a long time. If I can give this one thing to her, then I'll die fucking giving it to her.

I kiss her back with all of the hurt and love and pain and confusion that I've felt over these last few months. She moans into my mouth as our tears drip over our melded lips. Our tongues dance, slowly, passionately, and when I open my eyes, I'm staring right back into hers. She's with me. Right here. Right now.

No delusions because she's right.

This is real. It's the most real thing I've ever experienced in my life.

She's not just real.

She's everything.

I break the kiss, feeling dizzy from all the new emotions washing over me. I have to remind myself that this is for her as my cock strains against my zipper. I push on her chest until her back is flat on the sand and spread her legs, kneeling before her. I lick her from asshole to pussy over and over again. When I think she's almost there, I give her what she wants, licking and sucking on her swollen clit until she's screaming my name while she comes in a violent thrash, all the while her eyes are open and locked on me as if she closes them I'll be gone forever.

Just like they are.

"Please, Pike. I need you. I need you now," she says. Her eyes are clear, and the glazed look of delusion is nowhere in sight. She sits up and reaches for my belt releasing it from my jeans, then pushes them down my legs. I chuck them off while keeping eye contact the entire time. I reach for my shirt and pull it up over my head. Her hands immediately go to my chest. On instinct, I lift her up, setting her on top of me. "Take what you need."

"I need you," she says as I arch my neck and press my lips to hers.

"Then, take me," I offer. I lift her hips from my lap as she grabs my cock, positioning it at her pussy, then gradually release her until I'm buried inside the most wonderfully crazy girl I love.

She'd have to be crazy to want to be with me. Not in this way, but in any way.

The situation would be funny if it wasn't so devastatingly unfunny.

She groans and rocks her hips against me, causing the most beautiful friction up and down my shaft inside her tight wet heat. My eyes want to roll back in my head at the pleasure of it all, but I'd allow them to fall the fuck out before I let that happen and lose the connection we have.

She finds a pace and a rhythm, wrapping her hands around my head, threading her fingers through my hair while her perfect tits bounce in my face.

It's all too much and not fucking enough.

It will never be enough.

Not with Mickey.

Not ever.

"Pike, I need more," she begs, and I realize what she's asking, and she doesn't know how to get there herself.

I dig my fingers into her hips and raise her up until only the tip of my cock is inside of her. I thrust up, pistoling my hips as I drop her down. Over and over again, I fuck her and make her fuck me as we don't dare so much as blink.

It feels so right because it's with Mickey, but unlike the other times, it also feels all too wrong.

A tear rolls down her face as she comes, screaming and crying out through her orgasm as her pussy clenches around my cock so hard I almost come from how good it feels and how fucking painful it is.

I lick the tear off her cheek before it can reach her lips as I come long and hard inside of her. Spilling everything I have into her. Emotions, vulnerability, love.

"I fucking love you so much," I whisper as I regain my senses.

She stays on my lap with me inside of her. Our gazes finally break as her head collapses onto my shoulder. The blood rushes from my cock pulsing inside her pussy which is still constricting me like a vise I never want to get out of.

After a long while in the silence with nothing but the sound of our breathing and the occasional creaking of an old rocking chair on the porch behind us, she finally speaks. "I love you, too, Pike," I hear her strained whisper. "So, fucking much. It hurts. It all hurts so bad."

She sits up, pulling me from her body. She adjusts her shorts, and I pull up my pants. I feel the loss of her the second my cock slips from her body. I feel it everywhere. In my heart. In the air around us.

In my fucking soul.

Who knew that so much love would result in so much pain.

Mickey sobs. "Something is really, really wrong with me. I need help."

"Shhhh…it's okay. We will get you help," I say as her tears soak my shirt.

"I can't stay here," she says, digging her fingernails into the skin at the back of my neck.

"I know," I admit, resting my chin on her head. "It's okay. I know."

Mickey's loss, what she's been through, with her family dying, The Reich. I cringe.

What I've put her through.

I can't even begin to imagine all of it, never mind live it. It's no wonder that it's too fucking much for her to handle. No wonder she's breaking. If you punch a mirror, it's going to fucking break. Even one of the things she's been through would be too much for anyone else, but yet, for four years, she's marched on like a soldier who lost an arm and a leg in battle yet picked up his goddamned weapon and kept fucking fighting.

She's broken, and lost, but no matter what happens, she'll never be forgotten.

Not by me.

Not ever.

I'm shaking as I pull her even tighter to my chest. I close my eyes, and for once in my life, I allow the feelings to flow. The result is soaking her hair with my tears, silently crying for the girl I love. During this single moment, I allow myself to grieve.

Not just for myself.

Not just for her.

For what could have been.

"I love you, Mic," I whisper in her hair.

She turns to me with nothing behind her eyes. "Can I go see my sister now?"

18

PIKE

ONE YEAR LATER

MICKEY'S BEEN GONE for a year. In total, I knew her less than a month.

So then, why the hell am I so surprised when I called the treatment facility she's been living in to find that she completed her program and checked out over a week ago?

Where the hell is she?

I laugh to myself. Why the fuck did I automatically assume that she'd come here when her time there was up?

"Still can't find her?" Jo Jo asks, sliding up to me at the bar next to the pawn shop.

I shake my head and take a swig of my beer. "Nope. And you shouldn't be in here," I scold.

Jo Jo rolls her eyes. "Yeah, and I shouldn't have changed their sign to read *NUDE BAR FREE DRINKS*, but I did." She laughs. "And the look on Sally's face was totally worth it when those big burly nude guys came strolling up."

The kid has a point there.

Leave it to Jo Jo to pull a smile out of me when I didn't think it was possible. I don't think I would have made it through this past year without her to distract me from my own bullshit. Or, as Preppy would call it, wallowing.

With the help of Nine, I became Jo Jo's official guardian shortly after Mickey left.

The night I got arrested I promised Jo Jo she wasn't going back into foster care, and I fucking meant it. I'm a lot of things, but I'm not a liar.

I've learned that Jo Jo reminds me a lot of myself. Some of that is good, like the fact that she doesn't take shit from anyone, and some of it's downright terrifying, like her ability to manipulate me into pretty much getting whatever she wants.

Like, right now. I should be sending her back to the pawn shop, but she made me laugh, and I forgot all about the fact that Hanson's Bar is not exactly an appropriate place for a twelve-year-old kid.

"So, you gonna go find her, or what?" Jo Jo asks. She sits up on her knees on the stool and reaches behind the bar. She grabs a red plastic cup from a stack and the soda hose, filling the glass.

I narrow my eyes at her.

"Sorry," she says, sounding not all that apologetic. She raises her hands in defense. "I'm still getting used to this 'you're in charge of me and strongly discourage my terrible behavior' thing."

I take out my wallet and slap a few bills down on the bar. "Sally, for my beer and her soda," I say.

Jo Jo follows me out through the back door to the alley. "I'll bring back the cup!" she shouts back.

Sally smiles. She's used to Jo Jo's daily shenanigans by now and even helps Jo Jo do her homework at the bar before it opens.

"Pike, you didn't answer me, do you think she's coming back?"

I turn to face her. "I thought you didn't like Mickey?" I ask.

"I mean, she was okay. I like the way she didn't let me win at board games or video games. And she never talked to me like she felt sorry for me. The same way you don't. I wasn't a broken foster kid to her. I was just a kid. An asshole, but a kid." She shrugs. "It was nice for someone to see me for who I am but not make that all I am."

I put my arm around Jo Jo. For being so young, the kid has been through so much, and it's made her wise beyond her years. "Same, kid. And since you know I'd never lie to you, the truth is that Mickey might not be coming back."

"But you hope she does? Right?" her eyebrows shoot up.

"I sure as shit do. But I can hope all I want. It doesn't mean she's going to come back."

"I hope she comes back, too," she says.

I walk Jo Jo to the backdoor of my pawn shop and open it. She goes to duck under my arm, but a loud meowing stops her. She steps back out into the alley.

"The cats are fine. I already fed them," I say. "They're starting to be greedy little fuckers. Feed them three times a day every day for a year and get a vet to come out to spay and neuter and give them shots and keep them healthy and build a cat tower the size of the fucking Logan's Beach water tower filled with cat toys, and suddenly, you're the center of their universe and the owner of dozens of the little greedy fuckers."

"I wouldn't call them fuckers. More like, loveable nuisances."

The voice. It's not Jo Jo's. I know this voice.

"Holy shit," Jo Jo whispers, tugging on my shirt.

Slowly, I turn to where a woman on the other side of the alley is holding a small kitten in her arms. Long, dark hair draped over her shoulders. She's wearing a pair of white cut-off shorts and a blue t-shirt tied at her belly button. Holy shit is right.

Mickey. My Mickey.

"So, you two were talking about me?" Mickey asks, stepping toward us. She sets down the kitten who scurries off, disappearing into the cat tower.

"You're back," I say, my throat thick.

She beams up at me with clear determined eyes. "I'm back."

"For how long?" Jo Jo asks, as eager to hear the answer as I am.

Mickey steps toward us and looks at me when she answers. "For as long as you'll both have me."

I lift her in my arms and press my lips to hers. "Forever," I mumble into her mouth. "Fucking forever."

"Ew, I do not want to witness this shit," Jo Jo mutters, ducking into the shop. "Call me when you're done being gross."

The door shuts. I press Mickey against the wall. "How are you?" I ask, looking her over. She's here. She's really fucking here.

In every way.

She smiles and drops her forehead to mine, holding my face in her hands. "I'm great. I'm here."

"Where the fuck did you go? I called, and they said you left a week ago," I say.

"There were a lot of goodbyes I had to say. I held a different memorial every day for each member of my family. And I had to make sure that I was going to be able to handle life outside of treatment. I didn't want to come back and be a burden on you."

I hold her tighter. "You'd never be a burden. Never." I suck in a deep breath. "You came back to me," I say, still unable to believe she's real. That she's here in my arms. And I don't just mean here physically. I look deep in her eyes, and she knows what I'm trying to see. There's nothing dulling the light in her eyes.

She nods. "I didn't just come back. I came *home*."

My chest squeezes with everything I'm feeling, her words echoing happily in my brain.

Home.

"Why?" I ask. "You could have gone anywhere. Done anything—"

"I told you." Her eyes are glassy with happy tears. "You're my constant."

19

MICKEY

A Reason to Hate
By Dr. Michaela Lovejoy, Sc.D

REVENGE ISN'T QUICK, and neither is grief.

Just because I have some understanding of the way the mind works doesn't mean I could get mine to cooperate any better than someone who doesn't. It also doesn't mean I could avoid having to learn how to work through my grief.

In conclusion, I ask you this: What is truth?

Facts are truths, but people often don't see facts as finite. Truths are opinions often related to, but not founded in facts. Personal truths are not based on any sort of evidence but rather on beliefs cultivated into ideals.

Truth, at large, is based on opinion turned belief.

Religious followers believe that their ideologies are the truth. There are millions of religions in the world. When posed with the question of who is god—Or is there a god? Or what happens when we die?—a follower of each religion gives a different answer. However, the idea behind truth, is that only one of them can be correct, yet, stated differently, millions of people are wrong.

Therefore, the key to truth lies solely in the believer.

The same rings true for hate-based groups.

Creating a believer takes several elements. Some are biological. Some are the way humans are programmed as children along with a combined element of experiences that can be molded to shape around a belief. Personal attitudes associated with true or false ideals. That's what belief is. Chemicals and biology mixed with psychological circumstances. That's the potion for belief.

Manipulation can play a part in this but only if the subject is primed for psychological manipulation. Such as lacking an element of nurture is more likely to accept social influences changing their behavior or perception, as such, changing the very basis of what they see as truth, sometimes disregarding basic human understanding and widely known facts in order to achieve that belief.

If the subject is made or proved to feel like this truth creates better quality of life for them or motivates them in some way, either with a goal of something or fear of something, such as in social, religious, or ecumenical situations, the subject is much less likely to adapt to a new and more factual truth when confronted and will often offer explanations of why others became misinformed to the truth, rather than admit that theirs is unequivocally wrong.

When mental illness is presented in one's truth, it opens up the subject to a new kind of vulnerability which shapes the way the idea is seen, which, in cases of bipolar disorder or schizophrenia, appears to the subject as absolute and therefore, non-arguable. This makes manipulation of the subject difficult unless you find that social or ecumenical goal mentioned above.

On the day we are born, we begin our conditioning. Whether it's through our environment or through the people that surround us, we begin to form ideals and thoughts similar to their own. We figure out what is important in life often through what we see is important to others. If hatred is important to your family that becomes a part of your life. You wouldn't automatically agree that it's wrong because you've not experienced life outside that hate-filled world. And when you do, you take with you those ideals and make excuses for all that is good. You use broken logic to weave together pieces of a story that's missing chapters.

But there is hope. I learned that even if someone is conditioned to hate their entire lives. Who lived and breathed the words and ideals that have been planted in their young brains since birth, can change. The ideals are stuck in the brain with figurative super glue, and all they need to be dislodged is a solvent. Something to dissolve what's holding it inside.

And that solvent is love.

It took love for my subject to begin to reject his previous conditioning and start building his own sets of beliefs. His own life free from the binds of hatred. He's now free to love.

And so am I.

Real love isn't a fairy-tale. It's not what the influencers on social media show you. It can't be summed up by a pretty staged picture or by an all-out public declaration of devotion.

Real love isn't simple. And regardless of what you see out there in the world, it also isn't easy. The relationship that love emerges out of love takes hard work.

There are times when I want to strangle Pike, and I'm sure there are times he wants to strangle me (even outside of our bed). But the test for a solid relationship is not perfection. It's living every day thankful for the other person. It's knowing that in the big picture of life that this *person makes you want to be better. And through those heated moments, never ever doubting the love that brought you together.*

I've learned that there is no valid reason to hate. And that love isn't perfect, but it's real, and it's powerful enough to drive even the strongest hate from the heart.

Because love is the only truth that matters.

To subject P- Wherever you are, I hope you've found happiness within yourself. In turn, I hope that forgiveness has found you and that you've forgiven yourself. Thank you for teaching me that hate is not a mark that can't be erased.

"It's good, Mic. It's so fucking good." Thorne says, beaming up from the pages with pride. "What made you decide to turn your paper into a book?"

I glance over to Pike. "Well, someone told me that I couldn't let the information I learned die with the Reich and that what I did needed a greater purpose. And my purpose is to help. I needed to expose the Reich for what they were, and I needed to share my findings with the world. A paper wouldn't reach the masses, and so, this book was born. With this, I hope to educate and maybe even change a few minds out there."

Pike presses a kiss to my head. A silent expression of pride.

Thorne rushes from the room when the sound of the bell above the door chimes.

"Hey, kid," Preppy says, sauntering into the room, passing Thorne on his way in. "I just want to let you know that I always knew you were one of the good ones. Never lost faith in you. Not for one motherfucking second."

"Really?" Pike asks.

Preppy smiles. "It's true. You should ask the others. Actually, ask Ray and King how I got those two crazy kids together. It's a doozy of a story."

"Does it involve campaigning for their deaths?" I ask.

He smiles proudly. "No, but it involved a kidnapping and eventually resulted in my own death."

"What is he talking about?" I whisper to Pike.

He chuckles. "I'll tell you later."

"I tell you what," Preppy says. "Since you're a bonafide author now, the story would make for a really good book."

"Sure, I'll think about it," I say. Our cat, Greyson, meows at my feet, rubbing her fur against my ankle. Mindy's happy barking echoes throughout the pawn shop.

Jo Jo comes running down the stairs, wearing a pink dress and blue polka dotted leggings. "Is it here? Why didn't you guys fucking tell me!" she cries.

"Language," I warn.

Jo Jo smiles sheepishly.

With the help of Nine, who is a guardian of the court representing children in the system, our adoption of Jo Jo will be official in less than a week.

"Sorry, Mom," she sings. "But that's so super fucking cool."

I give her another stern warning, but it's hard to be actually mad at her when my heart feels like it's about to burst out of my chest with joy every time I see her. Every time I get to tuck her into bed. Every time she falls asleep while I'm reading her a book.

Pike winks at her. I give him a stern warning of his own. "What? Who decided which words are the fucking bad ones? Words are forms of expression, and I, for one, am not for the oppression or limitation of one's personal expression. It's not emotionally healthy."

Jo Jo and I both look at each other in shock and then turn to Pike. "You quoted her book!" Jo Jo cheers with a smile. She scrunches her nose. "Wait, Dad, I thought you hated reading?"

Pike frowns. "It's not that I hate reading. I have a reading disorder that makes me very frustrated when I read." He muses her hair. "But, I did listen to the audio version."

"That's genius!" Jo Jo exclaims, and I beam at the triumphant look in Pike's eyes as he picks Jo Jo up and spins her around the room. It takes a smart man to know and admit his limitations, and I managed to get myself the smartest of them all. If only more people could be like Pike. Selfless, understanding, and loyal without limits.

The world would be a much better place.

Preppy closes the book, then opens it again, flipping through the first few pages. "Have you seen this yet?" he asks Pike.

Pike puts Jo Jo down and peers over Preppy's shoulder. I know exactly what he's showing him, and I haven't yet told him about it myself. I watch his expression as he takes his time to read it to make sure he doesn't get the words jumbled.

He looks at me. "That's…" He nods, his expression a mixture of emotions. He clears his throat. "That's…we'll talk about it later. I think I just heard Thorne calling me. Come on, Jo Jo," he drags her out by the hand.

"Dad, I didn't hear anything? You high or something?" Jo Jo asks.

"What's got him in a rush?" Thorne asks, coming back in from the storage area with a box in her hand, obviously not having called Pike.

Preppy holds up the page so Thorne can read the words I wrote to thank the man who gave me my life back. A true purpose. The man I trust and will fight for with every day I have left on this earth.

FOR PIKE, I CHOSE LOVE BECAUSE YOU SHOWED ME HOW.

·

EPILOGUE
MICKEY

LOVE IS BIOLOGY. Neurochemicals, hormones, neuropeptides. They all have to align with testosterone, estrogen, dopamine, vasopressin, and oxytocin in order to produce the feeling of love. It's not an easy task which is why love—true love—is rare.

They are why I feel this bigger-than-myself love for Pike, Jo Jo, and Thorne. And this love is a feeling I trust more than anything. A reliable constant.

My truth.

Pike and I are walking down the beach. We are hand in hand with Jo Jo between us who switches between cursing at the seagulls and loudly pointing out the men wearing tiny speedos.

Our pace slows as we come upon the timeshare that I spent so many summers in with my family. The one that I fled to the night they were killed. The night I met Pike.

I glance up at the once boarded-up duplex where I spent so many happy summers. "I hope that whoever bought this place loves it as much as I do," I lament. "I spent a lot of happy times here."

Jo Jo runs ahead of us, chasing a crab in the sand. Mickey, the dog, chases her and then barks at the crab, punching her paws into the sand.

Pike takes my hand. "Your neighbor, the older lady, moved away to be with her kids. The other side was sold at auction. The same buyer picked up both halves and recently renovated it, combining the sides and making a decent three-bedroom two-bathroom house."

"That probably cost a fortune," I say. The once pink siding is now a more modern bright white. The shutters are black instead of the previous shade of faded purple. The wooden stairs and deck that was chipped and faded has been reinforced with strong beams crisscrossing underneath and freshly stained. The open spaces underneath that used to be for parking now houses a paver flooring and a huge outdoor kitchen with comfortable modern outdoor couches and tables. "It's beautiful. I'm jealous of whoever gets to live there."

"Because of your family?"

I squint against the sun and shade my eyes with my hand to get a better look at the house. "No, not just for the memories it holds, but because it's a gorgeous beach house."

Pike squeezes my hand. "And you're right, it did cost a fortune."

I twist my lips. "How do you know that?

He reaches into his pocket and holds up a key. "Because, I oversaw everything and because—" He hands me the key. "We own it now."

I turn the key over in my hand and look back to the house and then to Pike. "Are you serious?"

"I think you've figured out that my sense of humor doesn't extend to tricking you into believing I bought a house for us only to say, yeah, totally joking," he chuckles. "Besides, a one-bedroom apartment over the pawn shop isn't exactly enough room for a family of three. But it's perfect for Thorne. She's going to be moving in at the end of the week."

Mindy barks, chasing after Jo Jo.

"Family of four," he corrects. "Five, if you count the fucking cat."

"This is...I can't believe it." Pike is right about the apartment.

Jo Jo came to us from a situation where she didn't feel safe, and we wanted to do everything we could to make her feel that way, including giving her the bedroom with a door that locks. Which means that Pike and I have been sleeping on the pull-out couch. Lousy for both our backs and our privacy, but worth making Jo Jo feel comfortable.

"Why didn't you tell me!" I exclaim, slapping him in the chest. He holds my wrist to his chest.

"Because I didn't know how you'd feel about it, and I wanted to be sure," Pike says. "I wanted to know if this could be home for you. If you want. And I needed to know if..."

"If it was going to trigger me into losing my mind again?"

"I was going to say upset you, but sure, that works, too."

I've been working with therapists and counselors twice a week as well as attending a grief counseling group session once a week. Next month, I will begin leading my own group, and they won't be subjects. I won't be studying what makes them tick. My only goals will be to listen and to help. In addition, I'll be starting my own class in the prison system like the one Pike told me about. The kind that helps inmates leave gangs and groups like The Reich, but more importantly, I'll help teach them how to forgive themselves. How to love again.

Tears well up in my eyes. "You've already given me so much," I say, as Pike wipes a tear from my cheek with the pad of his thumb.

"Not nearly as much as you've given me," he replies.

I think he's about to kiss me when he bends over and scoops me up into his arms. I shriek in surprise and kick out my legs. "What are you doing?" I laugh.

"Mom! Dad!" Jo Jo calls from the porch. She sees Pike carrying me toward the house. "Does this mean we can show her now?"

"Yes!" I call up to her.

A sudden pricking at the back of my neck grabs my attention. "Can you put me down?" I ask Pike.

He frowns and sets me down.

"I'm okay," I assure him. "I just need a minute."

"I'll be by the steps when you're ready," he says, kissing my knuckles before dropping my hand.

I take a deep breath of salty air and then turn around to face the water. There on the shoreline is my family. My mother and father. Mallory, Mindy and Maya.

"It's okay to think about us, you know," Mallory says. "We are so happy for you!"

"We're okay where we are. We want you to be okay, too," Maya says.

My mother smiles. "It's okay to remember us. We're okay. None of this was ever your fault. We love you, and it's okay now that you remember we aren't here."

"I'm so sorry," my father says. "I did everything wrong, but not for

one moment during all of those horrible mistakes, did I ever not love you or your sisters."

"Yeah," Mindy butts back in. *"And if you don't live up to your full potential, I will haunt your ass for all of fucking eternity."*

"Language," my mother scolds, *just as I'd scolded Jo Jo earlier. I guess I know where I get it from.*

"Think of us, "my mother says. We will think of you. It's time for us to go now. Be happy, darling and know when you are that we are happy for you. Live your life and love with all of your heart the way I love you with all of mine.

My father stares at me with sad eyes.

"I forgive you," I whisper. I will never know my father's true heart or the reasons behind what he did, but people are complicated and my father was no exception. In order to let it go, I have to forgive.

And so I do.

Over the past two years, I've learned that carrying the weight of hate can crush a person, turn them into something they aren't. Moving on means being able to forgive and that's exactly what I want to do. Move on with Pike and Jo Jo.

"I love you all." I take a deep shaky breath. "Goodbye."

Pike comes up beside me and grabs my hand. "Everything okay?" he asks, his forehead lined with familiar concern.

I look up at him and then to the beach house where Jo Jo is waiting impatiently on the porch with her arms crossed and her foot tapping on the wood deck. Mindy, the dog, pokes her furry head through the posts of the railing, her pink tongue hanging out as she gives us a look that says she's just as impatient as Jo Jo.

"I'm great. I'm more than great. I'm happy." I smile. "Let's go home."

Pike takes me by the hand, and we trudge through the soft

sand. We reach the stairs, and I cast one last glance over my shoulder where the image of my family is fading as they smile until they're gone, disappearing into the waves, but never from my life. Because they're family.

And while people stop living, family never dies.

A NOTE TO MY READERS

Dear Readers,

I apologize with my entire heart for the delays in giving you this book. It was almost finished, and then...the apocalypse.

I'm not trying to give you excuses, just a few reasons.

Writing a book is hard.

Writing a book during the time of COVID-19 is super hard.

Writing a book in the wake of George Floyd's murder is beyond fucking hard.

Writing a book about a young white woman who is heavily involved in a white supremacist organization in the wake of COVID-19 and the murder of George Floyd has been the hardest ever.

While my heart has been heavy and my anxiety has run rampant, I've also been inspired.

And while my stories are pure fiction, I've delved deeper into some of these characters than I ever thought I would. I found out what makes them tick. I explored the idea of redemption and discovered what the line is that separates the redeemable from the non-redeemable.

My books are not political. They never have been. However, love and kindness aren't political ideals. They are instilled in us at birth, and it's only the influence of others that can tear those ideals down.

I invite you to think.

To ask questions.

To delve deeper.

To take one minute and ask yourself what you would do if you were in someone else's shoes.

Most of all, I invite you to love and be kind to one another.

We do not know what our fellow humans go through on a daily basis. What they suffer. What their real story contains within its pages. Why they act the way they do.

Our worlds are not everyone else's world.

Our beliefs are not absolute truths.

I'll leave you with this. It's a conversation I have with my five-year-old daughter every morning.

Me: Baby girl, what makes a happy heart?

Her: Kindness makes a happy heart, Mommy.

Me: And why is that?

Her: Because kindness is happiness!

Me: Exactly, baby. Exactly.

All my love and more.

WYTM,
TM Fraizer

ALSO BY T.M. FRAZIER

THE PERVERSION TRILOGY
PERVERSION (Book 1)

POSSESSION (Book 2)

PERMISSION (Book 3)

THE OUTSKIRTS DUET
THE OUTSKIRTS (Book 1)

THE OUTLIERS (Book 2)

THE KING SERIES
LISTED IN RECOMMENDED READING ORDER

Jake & Abby's Story (Standalone)

The Dark Light of Day (Prequel)

King & Doe's Story (Duet)

KING (Book 1)

TYRANT (Book 2)

Bear & Thia's Story (Duet)

LAWLESS (Book 3)

SOULLESS (Book 4)

Rage & Nolan's Story (Standalone)

ALL THE RAGE (Spinoff)

ABOUT THE AUTHOR

T.M. Frazier never imagined that a single person would ever read a word she wrote when she published her first book, The Dark Light of Day.

Now, she's a USA Today bestselling author several times over. Her books have been translated into numerous languages and published all around the world.

T.M. enjoys writing what she calls 'wrong side of the tracks' romance with sexy, morally corrupt anti-heroes and ballsy heroines.

Her books have been described as raw, dark and gritty. Basically, while some authors are great at describing a flower as it blooms, T.M. is better at describing it in the final stages of decay.

She loves meeting her readers, but if you see her at an event please don't pinch her because she's not ready to wake up from this amazing dream.

For more information please visit her website www.tmfrazierbooks.com

FACEBOOK: facebook.com/tmfrazierbooks

TWITTER: twitter.com/tm_frazier

INSTAGRAM: instagram.com/t.m.frazier

JOIN MY FACEBOOK GROUP, FRAZIERLAND: www.facebook.com/groups/tmfrazierland

Printed in Great Britain
by Amazon